# Giant on Horseback

Center Point
Large Print

Also by Lewis B. Patten and available from
Center Point Large Print:

*Lawless Town*
*Shadow of the Gun*
*Cañon Creek*
*Gun This Man Down*
*Savage Desert*

**This Large Print Book carries the
Seal of Approval of N.A.V.H.**

# Giant on Horseback

# Lewis B. Patten

CENTER POINT LARGE PRINT
THORNDIKE, MAINE

This Center Point Large Print edition
is published in the year 2017 by arrangement with
Golden West Literary Agency.

First US edition: Doubleday
First UK edition: Collins

The text of this Large Print edition is unabridged.
In other aspects, this book may vary
from the original edition.
Printed in the United States of America
on permanent paper.
Set in 16-point Times New Roman type.

ISBN: 978-1-68324-524-7 (hardcover)
ISBN: 978-1-68324-528-5 (paperback)

Library of Congress Cataloging-in-Publication Data

Names: Patten, Lewis B., author.
Title: Giant on horseback / Lewis B. Patten.
Description: Center Point Large Print edition. | Thorndike, Maine :
    Center Point Large Print, 2017.
Identifiers: LCCN 2017024364| ISBN 9781683245247
    (hardcover : alk. paper) | ISBN 9781683245285 (pbk. : alk. paper)
Subjects: LCSH: Large type books. | GSAFD: Western stories.
Classification: LCC PS3566.A79 G53 2017 | DDC 813/.54—dc23
LC record available at https://lccn.loc.gov/2017024364

# Giant on Horseback

# 1

Rain fell, gently drizzling, shining on the slicker worn by the stationmaster, dripping softly from the eaves of the weather-beaten, yellow-frame station. The train hissed patiently as it waited for the passenger to alight. A weathered sign proclaimed that the name of this place was SAN JUAN, NEW MEXICO.

It was a young man who stepped from the coach. He carried a single, well-worn carpetbag.

He was dressed in a dark business suit and wore a celluloid collar that stuck up an inch above the collar of his coat. He wore a black derby hat. The young man epitomized the very latest in fashion, this year of 1882.

He paused for an instant in the misting rain to stare north across the grass, at the mesas a dozen miles from town. Their tops and the upper part of their sheer rock rims were obscured by drifting clouds. Their rock faces were stained and darkened by streaks of moisture.

The train whistled shrilly and began to chug away. It cleared the station and the young man could look across the tracks at a buckboard with a slickered, dark-faced man on the seat. Plainly visible on the side of the buckboard was a brand, one that looked like a crude Mexican hat.

He turned his head to stare after the departing train almost regretfully, then stepped firmly off the platform and crossed the tracks. The dark-faced man glanced at him and the young man said, "I'm Morgan Lamb."

"Climb up. We got a long drive ahead of us."

Lamb dropped his bag into the back of the buckboard. He climbed up and the buckboard started with a jerk.

The driver turned his head. "Ain't you got a slicker?"

Lamb shook his head.

"You'll get soaked."

A faint smile touched the young man's wide mouth. He shrugged. "It's a warm rain."

The driver studied him a moment, almost uneasily. Then he drew the horses to a halt. He climbed down and rummaged under the seat. When he remounted it, he handed Lamb a folded tarpaulin. "You can put this around you. It'll keep you dry."

Morgan Lamb wrapped the tarpaulin around his shoulders. The driver extended a browned and callused hand. "I'm Pete Candelario. Your old man sent me to pick you up."

Lamb took the hand and gripped it. There was uncertainty in his steady brown eyes and there was doubt. There was also puzzlement. He had spent his life in Illinois and had no memories of this land where he had been born. He could remember neither his mother's nor his father's face. He had never seen a picture of either one of them.

Questions about them had always been avoided by his aunt and uncle. But now they both were dead and Morgan Lamb, who had turned nineteen yesterday, had come home to stay.

Candelario glanced aside at him as he started the buckboard and Morgan happened to catch the glance.

The things he surprised in the other's eyes served to further puzzle him. As though Candelario felt sorry for him.

Why? He frowned slightly. Because he had lost the two people who had been mother and father to him since he had been three? Or for something else?

Tall and solidly built, he sat rigidly straight on the buckboard seat. There was a day's growth of whiskers on his face. His jaw was long and hard, ending in a jutting chin. His cheeks were slightly hollow and his forehead was high and prominent.

An intelligent face, but a strong one too for a man so young. His eyes had a direct way of meeting Candelario's that made the other's shift unwillingly away.

The buckboard rattled across the tracks and entered the town. Now, Morgan got the smell of it, combining the odors of wet adobe, spicy Mexican cooking, manure, wet sagebrush, and

9

the slaughterhouse at the farthest edge of town.

It was a one-street town, lined with adobe buildings, some of which had false fronts and signs. Every third or fourth one seemed to be a saloon.

The last building on the street was the livery barn, tall, bulky, the biggest building in town. In front of it a group of men were inspecting a horse, passing a brown bottle among them as they did.

They stared at the buckboard and at Morgan Lamb as though they knew him or remembered him.

Candelario slapped the horses' backs with the reins, urging them to a trot. From behind, Morgan heard the words, ". . . even looks like him, by God! Now I know why Kehoe didn't want the son-of-a-bitch around."

He turned his head to glance at Candelario. The man's face was set and angry. His lips were compressed. He uttered a soft and bitter Spanish curse.

They left the town on a two-track road that wound steadily north to disappear into the mesas Morgan had noticed earlier. The rain slacked and stopped. Breaks appeared in the swift-scudding clouds and patches of sunlight appeared here and there on the land. The shafts of sunlight causing them were visible as rays because of the heavy moisture content in the air.

Once Morgan asked, more to break the tension than from curiosity, "How far is it?"

"All day. Part of the night. It's more'n a hundred miles. We'll change horses an' eat supper at my brother Juan's."

They drove in silence after that, sometimes shifting position on the seat to ease its hardness against their rumps. Morgan had earlier removed the tarpaulin and thrown it into the back.

He stared with interest at the endless, empty land, wondering that it could seem so completely new to him. He'd been three when he went away, but at three he could walk, and talk, and see. Yet he remembered nothing here.

Nagging questions troubled him. Why had his mother written but never his father? Why had his aunt and uncle avoided his questions about his father—as though the questions embarrassed them? And why did the eyes of Pete Candelario avoid meeting his directly, as though by so doing they would reveal something he did not want revealed? Why the remark back there in town and why had the remark angered Candelario the way it had?

Answers would come, of course, when he arrived tonight at the headquarters of sprawling Sombrero Ranch. He could wait until then.

Overhead the clouds continued to thin, and at last the sky was wholly blue. The sun warmed the land, made it steam and dry. Candelario slowed the horses to a walk.

He sat, taciturnly silent, staring unblinkingly at the road ahead. He volunteered no conversation and the hours passed.

There was no apparent change in the land, but in midafternoon a change came over Pete Candelario. From his indolent position on the buckboard seat he straightened. He glanced around. He seemed almost watchful as he drove.

Morgan glanced around too. He saw nothing, and relaxed again.

Pete did not. He sat very straight and continued to scan the country furtively.

When he reached under the seat for a rifle, Morgan followed the direction of his stare and saw five men ride out from behind a jutting point of land ahead.

Candelario continued to drive at the same pace, now with the rifle across his knees.

Morgan asked, "Something the matter?"

"Nothin' I can't handle. Just sit tight."

"What's it about?"

"No harm in your knowin', I guess. That's Luke Parfet and some of his men. This is his land we're on. He an' Clint Morgan ain't got much use for each other, so Luke claims he's closin' this road to Clint."

"Can he do that?"

Pete shrugged. "He can try."

12

The men ahead stopped while the buckboard was still a couple of hundred yards away. Pete stopped the buckboard immediately and watched impassively as they approached.

One of the men asked, "Who you got there, Pete?"

"Kehoe Lamb's kid. Get out of the road, Luke."

"It's my road an' it's my land. It's closed to you."

"Get out of the road, Luke. Don't be a fool. Clint . . ."

Luke interrupted. "Clint can go to hell!" He shifted his glance to Morgan. "He don't look much like Kehoe, does he, Pete?" Luke said.

Puzzled, Morgan glanced at Candelario's face. It had lost color. The man's lips were set angrily. But he did not reply. He only repeated his demand. "Get out of the road."

"Huh-uh. Can he talk, Pete?"

Morgan didn't understand the implications of Luke's words. But he did understand the studied insolence in his tone. "I can talk. What do you want to know?" Morgan said.

Luke's pale eyes settled on Morgan's face. He was blocky and powerful, but running to paunch. Like Morgan he needed a shave. His face was blotchy and veins stood out prominently on his forehead. He was dressed in range clothes and wore a gun. He asked harshly, "What's your name?"

"Morgan Lamb."

Luke grinned delightedly, but there was pure wickedness in his eyes. He turned his head and shouted, "That's it, boys! It's Clint Morgan he reminds me of—not Kehoe Lamb!"

They echoed his laughter. Morgan stepped down from the buckboard seat. Anger was rising in him, not because he fully understood but because he knew they were taunting him. The dispute might be over the road and the right-of-way, but he was being used as the goat. He said, "If you've got something to say, say it. If you want a fight, get off your horse and I'll try to accommodate you."

Luke roared, "Feisty rooster, ain't he? Mebbe we oughta take some of that out of him before we send him on home to Clint." The laugh died suddenly and his voice turned icy. "Put that gun down, Pete! Fire a shot an' you an' him will both be dead!"

Pete lowered the rifle reluctantly. His face was gray. He said, "Clint will . . ."

"I don't give a damn what Clint Morgan does! Watch Pete, boys."

He returned his attention to Morgan. He reined his horse closer. Suddenly his boot lashed out, its high heel catching Morgan on the side of the face. The spur raked his neck and blood sprang from the cut.

Groggy and scarcely conscious, Morgan staggered back. He fell. For the briefest instant he laid still while his anger grew, while the unprovoked injustice of the attack fed its leaping flames. Luke, still astride his horse, reined close and waited for Morgan to get up, boot poised for a second kick.

And now, even more than the attack had done, Luke's contemptuous attitude infuriated Morgan Lamb. He came to his knees.

The horse fidgeted, made uneasy by the smell of blood. Morgan lunged to his feet, seizing Luke Parfet's boot as it swung toward his head.

Holding on, he flung himself back, letting his weight dump Luke from the saddle. The man hit the ground on his back and grunted heavily as the air was forced from his lungs.

Morgan released the boot and came to his feet. Luke fought his way to his knees and stayed that way, gasping desperately for air, retching, sweating heavily.

Morgan swung a wild right that collided with the side of his head and knocked him rolling. He leaped after Luke, came down astride the man and began pummeling his face savagely.

Out of a corner of his eye, he saw a horseman approaching, but he did not look up. A rope settled over his shoulders. He felt himself yanked away from Parfet.

He clawed at the rope helplessly, without

15

success. It pinned his elbows against his body like iron.

His sense of motion increased. The sky and earth whirled before his eyes. Dust and grit filled his nostrils, his mouth and eyes. The clothes shredded from his back.

The man dragging him was galloping in a circle. The others yelled encouragement.

A sudden shot. The dragging stopped as abruptly as it had begun. A man began to curse, viciously, endlessly.

Morgan flung the rope off and struggled to his feet. Knuckling his eyes, he stood, gasping, grunting with pain. When his vision cleared, he saw Pete standing beside the buckboard, rifle leveled at the four who had accompanied Luke. A horse, the one that had been dragging him, lay kicking on the ground. Luke was just getting up, and his face was sick.

The tables were turned. The three had probably been so engrossed with watching Morgan being dragged that they'd forgotten to keep an eye on Pete . . .

"Shed your guns, the bunch of you!" Pete said.

Morgan staggered to the buckboard and stood there, hanging onto the seat. He heard the men's guns and belts thud against the ground. Pete said, "Feel like gatherin' up them guns?"

Morgan nodded dumbly. He stumbled to where

the guns lay and gathered them up, one by one. Pete said sharply, "You too, Luke. Drop it and step away!"

Morgan dumped the four guns and belts into the buckboard then crossed to Luke and picked his up. Straightening, he glanced at the man, surprising a look of hatred in Luke Parfet's eyes that, for an instant, turned him cold. He walked to the buckboard and dumped Parfet's gun in the back with the others.

Pete Candelario said, "We'll drop off these guns when we leave your land. If you get within rifle range of me again, I'll open up."

Morgan climbed wearily to the buckboard seat. The rig began to move.

Pete's voice was softer now. "Hold on, kid. We'll be at Juan's place in an hour. His old woman's a whiz at fixin' a man up after a fight."

In spite of Morgan's exhaustion and pain, he was now beginning to understand both Luke's taunts and the remark he had overheard in town. And understanding, everything else was suddenly stark and clear.

He was not the son of Kehoe Lamb. He was the son of someone named Clint Morgan. Or at least that was what everybody believed.

He wished suddenly that he had never come. Because he was going to be hated here—not for what he was or for anything he had done, but because Clint Morgan was hated and because everybody believed he was Clint Morgan's son.

Through the exhaustion—through the pain—his anger began to stir again. He was here and he would stay. They had hurt him and by so doing had made him a part of whatever was going on.

# 2

Juan Candelario's place nestled against a low hill. It was built of adobe and partially dug into the side of the hill, probably for warmth in winter. The hill faced south.

A gallery ran the width of the house in front, supported by grayed and weathered spruce poles over a foot thick. The house was thatched with sod, out of which grew a profusion of grass and weeds corresponding to those growing out of the hillside behind it. The windows were barred, tending to give it the appearance of a jail.

As they drove into the yard, Pete said, "I was born in that house. So was Juan. The Comanche tried to take it three times, but they never got the job done because we made it too expensive for them. An Injun'll quit when his losses start gettin' big."

There was a corral a couple of hundred yards beyond the house, where a draw carried a small stream of water. It was channeled by means of wooden troughs both into the corral and to the side of the house, where it made a wet, muddy spot spilling onto the ground.

Dried peppers hung from strings in the gallery's shade. A broken-down wagon weathered patiently beside the corral. There were several horses in the corral, and a buckboard beside the wagon that looked usable. Several saddles rested on the top pole of the corral.

A man came into the yard as the buckboard drew to a halt. He resembled Pete, his brother, except that he was very fat. He wore a wide-brimmed sombrero, a dirty white shirt open halfway to his navel, and a shapeless pair of cotton trousers secured at the waist by a piece of cotton rope. His bare feet were dirty and very brown.

A gold tooth gleamed in the sunlight as he grinned at Pete and at Morgan Lamb. He said, "*Bienvenidos*, Señor Lamb," and launched into a stream of Spanish that Morgan didn't understand. Pete replied, also in Spanish, and Juan nodded his head ponderously. His eyes sharpened as they studied Morgan's face.

Then, in English, he said, "Get down, señor. My house is yours."

Morgan dismounted stiffly from the buckboard. He followed Juan into the house.

It was filled with delicious, spicy odors of cooking meat. There were two women in the enormous living room, which also served as a kitchen. One was obviously Juan's wife. She was about his age, and equally fat. The other was young, slender, dark of hair and eye. She studied Morgan furtively as he came in, but dropped her glance shyly when he met it with his own.

Juan spoke rapid Spanish to his wife for several moments. She left the stove and crossed the room to Morgan, clucking, drying her hands on a towel. She pushed him gently into a chair and turned her head to issue several sharp commands to the girl in Spanish. The girl brought a pan of hot water, a washcloth, and soap. The older woman helped Morgan out of his shirt.

There were bloody abrasions on both shoulders and elbows, and one the size of his hand on the left side of his chest. He gritted his teeth as she washed them.

She said, "Your trousers, señor. Take your trousers off."

He felt his face grow hot and glanced at the girl. She giggled and turned her back.

The woman loosened his trousers and before he knew what she was doing, raised his feet and yanked them off. The girl turned her head and giggled again.

Morgan said, "Damn it . . ."

Grinning at him, Pete said, "No use to struggle, boy. That woman always gets her way."

Already she was bathing the long, bloody abrasions on the sides of his thighs. When she had finished, she patted some kind of ointment on them. She left and returned, carrying a clean pair of cotton trousers, a cotton shirt and a pair of straw sandals. Morgan put them on.

The girl brought him a basin filled with hot water and began to wash dust and blood from his face. One side of his mouth was smashed and one eye swelling, preparatory to turning black. The spur gash on his neck burned like fire. The girl's eyes were teasing until Morgan met her glance with his own steady one. Then she flushed and avoided his eyes. Watching, Juan Candelario laughed uproariously, which further increased the girl's confusion.

Juan said, "That one is Pete's daughter, Morgan. Her name is Ellen. Elena in the Spanish, but she likes Ellen best. She came with Pete last night."

Ellen finished and handed Morgan a towel. He dried his face, feeling better, feeling the friendship of these people as plainly as he had felt the hostility of the five who had intercepted the buckboard earlier.

He got up and walked to the door as Juan's wife began to set the table for dinner. He went out and Pete Candelario followed him. He wished he could question Pete, but he instinctively understood that it would be a mistake.

No one could tell him the things he had to know. He would have to find them out for himself. But he could ask about Sombrero, and did. "Tell me about Sombrero. How big is it?"

Pete laughed. He spread both arms wide, gesturing in all directions. "A million and a half acres. It is a day's ride to cross it, a week's ride to go around its boundaries."

"How did one man ever get that much land?"

Pete laughed again. "You do not know Clint Morgan, señor, or you would not ask."

For an instant, Morgan stood staring at him dumfoundedly. He didn't know exactly where he had gotten the idea, but he had thought Sombrero was owned by Kehoe Lamb.

Pete didn't seem to notice. He said, "The part of it that the buildings are on was once a grant from the Spanish king. How Morgan got it has always been the subject of much talk, but no one really knows. The rest of it . . ." He shrugged eloquently. "He got it the way Clint Morgan gets everything."

"And how is that?"

Pete shrugged. "You will know that when you have met Clint Morgan, señor."

"And my father . . . Kehoe Lamb. What . . . ?"

"What does he have to do with it? He is Morgan's foreman. He is as much a part of Sombrero as Morgan is himself. He has been here since I was a little baby in that house back there. He was here before the war, and when it was over he came back. He has been here ever since."

More than anything else, Morgan wanted to ask how Kehoe Lamb could stay, could take orders from Clint Morgan, could see him every day, knowing the things that were being said . . .

Morgan shook his head almost angrily. He didn't know those things were true. All he had to go on were the taunting insinuations of the five who had intercepted the buckboard. And the remark he had overheard in town.

From the house, Juan Candelario called them for supper and they went inside. The three men sat down at the table. The women did not sit down until the men were served.

Afterward, Pete and Juan went out to change horses. Morgan followed. Juan's wife said something in Spanish to Ellen and she, too, went outside.

The air was soft and warm. The sun was almost down. It laid a sheen of gold upon the few high clouds, a cast that was almost orange upon the faces of the mesas to the east.

Morgan walked stiffly across to the corral. Inside, Pete and Juan had caught fresh horses. They bridled them, changed harness from the first team to this one, then led them out and across to the buckboard. Morgan turned to follow, colliding with Ellen, who was right behind him, as he did.

He said surprisedly, "I'm sorry."

"*De nada.* It is nothing." She flushed as he

23

studied her face. Then her eyes met his, serious, determined. "Do you know what you are getting into?"

He frowned faintly, unsure of his own readiness to explore the subject yet, a little embarrassed that she should know what was being said about his origin. At last he nodded reluctantly. "A little, I think." He studied her face, and her glance lowered. She was changed from the girl who had giggled and flirted back inside Juan Candelario's house. He said, "There were some men in front of the livery stable back in town. I overheard something as we passed . . ." He stopped a moment. "Then later, when Luke Parfet stopped us . . . they made it pretty plain. I'm supposed to be Clint Morgan's son and not Kehoe Lamb's."

She nodded, still refusing to meet his glance.

"Do I look like Morgan?" he asked bluntly.

She nodded. "Like he must have looked when he was young."

"Then you think it's true?"

"I don't know. Mr. Lamb must believe it. Your mother . . ."

He interrupted. "What's she like?"

The girl's face softened. "You'll have to meet her. I can't tell you. But she's wonderful." Her face clouded. "If she made a mistake, she's paid for it."

"If it's true, how can Kehoe Lamb stay on? Why doesn't he go away?"

24

The girl's mouth firmed angrily. "If he went away, he might have to forgive your mother. He might not have anything to hate if he stopped seeing Clint Morgan every day."

"If he hates Morgan that much, why doesn't Morgan send him away?" He instantly knew the answer to that from the expression on Ellen's face. Clint Morgan was still in love with Kehoe's wife. And if Kehoe left, he would take her away with him.

Morgan Lamb leaned wearily against the corral fence. If he had known . . .

"Don't go there, Morgan," Ellen said softly. "Go back. Go anywhere. No one deserves what will happen to you at Sombrero. Kehoe will hate you. Your being there will hurt your mother. And everyone who hates Clint Morgan will hate you too."

From the direction of the house he heard Pete shout, "Ellen! Morgan! Let's go!"

He pushed himself away from the corral. He looked down at Ellen's face, remembering how soft, how warm her body had felt as he collided with her earlier. He remembered the way her hands had felt against his skin as she had washed the cuts on his face.

Her eyes met his and clung. Then suddenly she was gone, running back toward the waiting buckboard in front of the house.

He followed, walking awkwardly because of

pain caused by the rubbing of his clothes against the raw places on his legs. When he reached the buckboard, Pete and Ellen were already on the seat. He climbed up beside Ellen, who avoided his eyes. He called out his thanks to Juan and his wife as the buckboard started.

The sun was now wholly down and the glow had faded from the clouds. The sky was uniformly gray.

The miles dropped away behind. Stars came out, winking brightly in a cloudless sky. The air cooled and grew chill.

Morgan knew when they were drawing near because the team stepped up its pace. And at last he saw it in the distance, like a town, spread out across the plain in front of him.

He felt his chest constrict until it was painful just to breathe. There was no eagerness in him, no anticipation. There was only dread.

The people there were strangers to him. Yet he understood that his own life was and would be closely interwoven with theirs.

He must be part of their loves, their hatreds, their conflicts and triumphs. As they drove into the gate, he felt Ellen's small hand close over his own, as though she understood his thoughts. Then he was climbing down and staring at the dark, forbidding house.

# 3

The arrival of the buckboard must have been heard, for almost immediately a lamp flickered alive in a room at one end of the long gallery and a moment later, another glowed directly ahead in what must have been the living room.

Morgan started toward the main door, but stopped as a woman's voice called out from the end of the long gallery, "Morgan? Is that you?"

Pete said softly, "That's your mother, Morgan. She and Kehoe have that part of the house. Go ahead and see her. I'll go in and talk to Clint."

Morgan limped hesitantly along the dark gallery. He could see the slender shape of a woman ahead of him.

Suddenly it seemed almost impossible for him to go on. Any way you looked at it, this was an impossible situation. His mother was calling to him from the end of the gallery, but his mother was a stranger to him and he a stranger to her. His father—his real father—was in that other room, also a stranger, waiting to see what this bastard son of his looked like.

And where was Kehoe Lamb? Was he waiting to see Morgan too or was he sitting in a saloon

27

someplace getting drunk? Morgan thought that if he had been Kehoe Lamb that was what he would have been doing.

The trouble was, he knew none of these people. He didn't know where lay the right and wrong. He didn't know his own feelings, except that he wished he hadn't come because he dreaded meeting his mother, dreaded with equal intensity meeting his father and Kehoe Lamb.

But he continued along the gallery until he reached her.

She stood as though frozen for a moment, staring up into his face hungrily. Then, in a voice so faint he scarcely heard, she said, "Come inside, Morgan. Come inside where I can look at you."

At least, he thought as he followed her inside, she hadn't tried to embrace or kiss him. At least she had recognized the strangeness that was inevitable between them.

Inside, she turned. Tears brimmed from her eyes and ran across her cheeks silently. Her mouth trembled.

She was scarcely taller than Ellen. She wore a wrapper made of some heavy woolen material with a collar of snowy white. She was younger than he had imagined she would be, but there were lines in her face . . .

She was smiling . . . Her lips were trembling . . . The tears continued to flow silently across her cheeks. He was reminded suddenly of a late afternoon sun shining brightly from the west while clouds overhead continued to pour down rain.

She said softly, "Morgan. Morgan. How I've wanted to see you. It has been so long . . ." Her hands went suddenly to her face and a sob shook her. Then they came down and she was smiling at him again.

He felt his own throat constrict, his own eyes begin to burn. And he understood for the first time what torment it must have been for her, living out her life deprived of her only child.

He crossed to her suddenly, took her face between his hands, bent and kissed her lightly on the mouth. And suddenly her restraint disappeared. Sobs shook her, a weeping that was almost hysterical.

He held her close, surprised at her frailty. He felt as though he could scarcely breathe. In that instant, he hated a man he had never seen. He hated Kehoe Lamb.

After a long while, she drew away. "I'm sorry, Morgan. I wasn't going to do that. I know it must embarrass you."

He couldn't speak. She said, as though understanding this, "You must be starved. And tired. And you've been hurt, haven't you?" Her eyes, which had previously noticed none of his hurts, were suddenly filled with concern.

He said hoarsely, "Nothing serious. Juan Candelario's wife fixed me up."

"Did you fall from the buckboard? You look almost as though . . ." Her face suddenly paled. Her eyes took on a stricken look.

Wanting more than anything to spare her, he said, "It was something about the right-of-way across Luke Parfet's land. A fight. But I'm not hurt. I'm really not."

The relief in her face made him glad he had lied. She knew he would find out someday, he realized. But she didn't want him to know just yet. Not now. Not at this moment of reunion.

She said, "I'll fix you something to eat. And the coffee's hot."

"That sounds good."

"Come on out in the kitchen then." She turned and hurried through a door. He heard her strike a match. She was lowering a lamp chimney as he came through the door.

He glanced around. It was a nice kitchen, with windows looking out, he supposed, to the rear of the house. Apparently this was a separate dwelling even though it was connected to the main house.

He watched her move almost frantically around as she prepared a meal for him. And he found himself wondering how it had happened and why. She was not the kind of woman to be unfaithful to her husband. Did she still love Clint

Morgan? She must have loved him once . . .

And when had it happened? In what year? He was nineteen now . . . He had been born in 1863 . . . He had been born the second year of the war.

That was it, of course. Kehoe Lamb had gone away to war, Pete had said.

Not that it really excused anything. He watched her move about the kitchen, wanting to ask so many questions of her but knowing he could ask none of them.

She fried ham, eggs, and potatoes. She cut him an enormous piece of apple pie. He ate hungrily while she sat across the table and watched his every move.

There was a knock on the gallery door and she left him briefly. When she returned she said, "Mr. Morgan would like to see you. But finish eating first."

He gulped the last of the coffee. "I'm finished." He avoided looking at her, not wanting to surprise any unguarded emotions in her eyes. He experienced a certain dread of seeing Clint Morgan but he knew it had to be done. The man was his father though it was doubtful if he was going to acknowledge it.

He got to his feet. She said, "There is a room here for you. It's all ready."

He nodded. "I won't be long." He found himself wishing he had not ruined his clothes in the fight. He was at disadvantage enough without appearing before Clint Morgan in loose cotton shirt and trousers and straw sandals. He found himself resenting Morgan before he even reached the door.

He went out onto the dark gallery and walked along it toward the main part of the house. His resentment toward Morgan grew.

The courtyard was deserted now. The buckboard was gone and so were Pete and Ellen. Something cold was in Morgan's chest as he knocked on the thick front door.

The voice from inside was muffled but understandable. "Come in. Come in!"

He opened the door and stepped inside. The size of the room first impressed his consciousness. It was enormous, and must have had a ceiling twelve feet high.

But even standing in so large a room, the man he faced was huge. Taller than Morgan by a couple of inches, he was deep of chest and enormously broad in the shoulders.

The light in the room was poor. Morgan stepped closer. The other man picked up the lamp and came toward him, holding it high so that he could see.

It illuminated his face, and Morgan stopped cold in his tracks. He was looking at a face that might be his own face twenty-five years from now.

He said harshly, "I'm Morgan Lamb," trying to keep the challenge out of his voice, not entirely successful in doing so.

He could hate this man. It would not be hard. Because Clint Morgan was overpowering.

His jaw was long, his chin jutting. He had apparently not shaved today, for his face was covered with a stubble of graying whiskers. His eyes, sunken deep below monstrously bushy brows, were penetrating and hard.

An arrogant, ruthless man. Those characteristics stood out in Clint Morgan and were as noticeable as his size. He growled, "What the hell happened to you?"

Morgan clenched his jaws. He stared straight into the older man's eyes. "I had a fight with one of your neighbors. Luke Parfet. He didn't want to let us use his road."

"Whip him?"

"I suppose you might say I did. Does that make you feel good?"

"Don't get smart with me, boy."

"Why not?" Morgan felt suddenly reckless. And angry. And resentful too. Let Clint Morgan spell out the truth for him right now.

The big man froze. For an instant he stood utterly motionless, staring at Morgan. Then his shoulders sagged. He said, "You hate me already, don't you? I had hoped . . ."

"What had you hoped?"

Clint Morgan didn't answer the question directly. "You know I'm your father, don't you?" he said.

"I know."

"Is that all you know?"

"Isn't it enough?"

"No, by God, it isn't enough! You've met your mother. You've seen what kind of woman she is. If you condemn me, you condemn her too."

Morgan didn't speak. He didn't know what to say. Clint turned his back and crossed to a heavy oaken straight-backed chair. He sat down and put the lamp on the floor in front of him. He took bottle and glass from the table beside him and poured the glass half full. He drank the liquor like water. "Want one?"

Morgan shook his head. He walked into the middle of the room and stood there, staring at Clint.

At last Clint said, "Kehoe Lamb and your mother were married the day before Kehoe left for Fort Union. He didn't get back for three years."

He was silent for a long, long time. His face, illuminated by the lamp on the floor in front of him was less harsh than it had been before. He stared straight ahead of him as though seeing things Morgan would never see.

Almost reluctantly he said, "I was in love with

her before she and Kehoe were married. I never changed. And with Kehoe gone . . . with no more than the two of them had had . . . She fell in love with me. What happened . . . well, that's all. It was my fault much more than hers. But it never happened again."

His face hardened suddenly. "I'd have done anything to keep her. I might even have killed Kehoe when he came back. Except that I knew if I did she would leave and I'd never see her again. I almost did kill him anyway the day he sent you away. I may someday kill him yet. Because he has punished her every hour of every day for the last seventeen years."

"You'd like it if I hated him, wouldn't you?" Morgan was ashamed of that almost as quickly as he finished saying it. He knew it was childish.

But Clint didn't seem to think it was. He said, "He hates you, boy. He's hated you all your life even though you weren't here. It wasn't only Kehoe that sent you away. It was your mother too. Because she knew Kehoe's hatred would ruin you."

He poured himself another drink. This time he poured the glass full and again he drank it as though it were water. He coughed, fished in his pocket for a cigar and lighted it. His fingers shook violently.

Almost as though talking to himself, he said, "I've fought. All my life I've fought. For this

35

ranch. For cattle. For money and power. And it's no good. It isn't what I wanted at all."

Morgan didn't speak because he didn't know what to say. The silence dragged on until he thought Clint had forgotten he was there. Clint's eyes had an almost vacant look in them as though his thoughts were far away. At last Morgan said, "I . . . I'll probably see you tomorrow."

Clint looked up. "Are you going to stay? I wouldn't blame you if you didn't."

Morgan said, "I don't know. I don't know yet what I'll do."

He turned, crossed the room and went out the door, closing it behind him. He stood for an instant in the blackness of the gallery.

He knew if he stayed on here, he was a fool. He also knew that if he didn't stay, it would be because he was afraid.

# 4

When he awoke in the morning, the sun was well up in the sky. Someone was knocking on his door, and as he sat up, his mother entered with an armload of clothes. "I found some things— of Kehoe's—that I thought you could wear." She smiled at him hesitantly, searching his face anxiously. Then she turned and hurried from the room.

36

He stood up and stretched, frowning. She must know that he had noted the resemblance between himself and Clint Morgan. It was unmistakable. She was probably wondering how much he had guessed. And she was tortured with the wondering.

He dressed quickly. He went out into the kitchen where she was preparing breakfast for him. The word "mother" came unfamiliarly to his lips but he said, "Mother, I know. I know whose son I am."

She froze, her back to him, looking small and helpless and defenseless.

His throat was so tight he could scarcely speak, "I'm not a judge and it happened almost twenty years ago. Whatever you did . . ." He couldn't finish, but she understood. She turned. Tears were streaming from her eyes. She didn't move toward him, but in her face, in her eyes were things . . .

He turned his face away, his own eyes burning fiercely. He walked to the window and stared outside. He wished he were someplace else, and yet he was glad that he was here.

Very softly, her voice trembling, she said, "Kehoe will be back soon. He'll show you around."

He nodded, turned, and sat down at the table. She brought him a cup of coffee. Each avoided the other's eyes.

In spite of that—there was a new warmth and closeness between them—a thing of feeling—unspoken . . .

He thought of Kehoe Lamb. He would hate Kehoe Lamb. He would accept nothing from Lamb, nor would he accept anything from Clint Morgan. If he couldn't earn his way he'd leave.

He was still stiff and sore from the fight and the dragging yesterday, but not so much so as he had been last night. The abrasions on his thighs and shoulders were scabbed, and if nothing broke the scabs they would quickly heal.

He was finishing breakfast as someone noisily yanked a plunging horse to a halt in the courtyard outside. His mother hurried through the house toward the front door, Morgan followed.

She opened the door, but almost immediately turned away from it, her face pale, her eyes frightened. He heard a man's voice yell, "Mary! Where is he, Mary?"

Morgan pushed her aside and stepped onto the sun-washed gallery. He closed the door behind him.

This had to be Kehoe Lamb, and Lamb was drunk. He was so drunk he swayed in his saddle. He stared at Morgan furiously for several long moments. Then he growled, "Yeah. The spittin' image. You look enough like him to be his son." He laughed harshly at his own sour joke.

Anger stirred in Morgan. Anger that crawled

38

and consumed like fire in a loft of hay. Kehoe roared, "Well, don't just stand there! Say somethin'!"

Morgan stared up at him coldly. Kehoe was a tall man, thin. A big-framed man, but his eyes were deeply sunken into their sockets and his brows, heavy and unkempt, added to the impression of depth. His face was unshaven, his mouth slack with the liquor he had consumed. But his eyes burned with hatred, hatred fed by carefully nurtured resentment and wounded male pride.

Why hadn't he left her? Morgan wondered. Why had he stayed on all these years, torturing her, torturing himself, torturing Clint Morgan? He knew the answers to these questions almost before his mind finished asking them. Staying had been Kehoe Lamb's revenge.

He had stayed and had tried to destroy his wife. He had tried to destroy Clint. It was pretty plain, even to Morgan, that he had succeeded only in destroying himself.

Morgan didn't know what to say. He wouldn't be pleasant. He wouldn't ignore the things Kehoe had said to him. Nor did he want to fight with Kehoe, particularly when the man was drunk, particularly here and at this time. So he remained silent, and his silence seemed to further infuriate the man staring down at him from the back of the sweaty, winded horse.

Morgan met his glance steadily. Staying here, he realized, was impossible for him. He couldn't stay with Kehoe hating him. Remaining would only add to his mother's unhappiness because his continued presence would be a reminder to Kehoe—of what had happened twenty years ago.

"God damn you, say something!" Kehoe roared. "Open your mouth! Let's see if you sound as much like him as you look like him!"

For the briefest instant Morgan felt pity for the man. Then it was gone. Kehoe had been wronged, but that had been twenty years ago. Kehoe had revenged himself a thousand times over until vengeance had become his way of life.

Kehoe's face turned almost purple with balked fury. He started to swing from his horse.

Morgan knew that if he ever got off the horse there would be a fight. Right here in front of his mother's door he would have to whip Kehoe or be whipped himself.

He flung his arms out suddenly. He yelled explosively at Kehoe's horse.

The animal shied away, and whirled. Morgan brought the flat of his hand down hard against the animal's rump.

Nervous anyway from the hard ride Kehoe had given him, the horse plunged away, with Kehoe instinctively keeping his seat. Man and horse disappeared through the courtyard gate.

Morgan turned his head. He saw Clint Morgan

standing on the gallery in front of his own door, scowling.

The young man turned and walked that way. "I can't stay here," he said. "You can see that. I'll leave today."

For an instant there was shock in Clint's seamed face. Then it was gone as the man nodded ponderously. "I can see it. But where will you go?"

Morgan shrugged. He had no idea where he would go. Any place but here.

"Let me give you a horse. And some money . . ."

Morgan said, "I'll borrow a horse from you. I'll leave him at the livery stable in town."

Clint nodded with grudging approval. Morgan turned and walked back along the gallery to where his mother was waiting for him. "I'm going to leave," he said. "I have to. I'll let you know where I am, and I'll write to you."

She nodded dumbly, her face stricken.

He said impulsively, "Come with me. Don't stay here with him."

She shook her head. "He is my husband."

He saw instantly that argument would be useless. Staying was her penance—for the wrong she had done Kehoe so many years before.

Morgan suddenly wanted to be gone—to be away from here quickly. He crossed the courtyard and went through the gate. Kehoe was nowhere in sight.

North of the main house there was a small stream lined with cottonwoods. Along this stream were a number of adobe houses. Downstream from the houses there was a corral in which there appeared to be nearly a dozen horses. Morgan walked toward it. He'd catch and saddle a horse. He'd return to the house long enough to tell his mother good-bye and get his bag. Then he'd go.

He was almost to the corral when he heard running footsteps behind him. He turned.

Ellen Candelario was running after him. He stopped and waited until she caught up. "How was it, Morgan? How did it go?" she asked breathlessly.

He grinned unconvincingly. "Not too bad."

"Where are you going?"

"I'm leaving. Staying here will only make things worse."

Her eyes held regret. "I'm sorry. I was hoping you would stay."

For an instant they stood looking steadily at each other. Morgan felt a stir of attraction. Resisting it, he said, "I'd better catch a horse."

"Can you . . . ? I mean . . ."

He grinned. "They have horses in Illinois. Sometimes people even ride them."

She flushed faintly. He took a rope from the corral gate, stepped inside and selected a horse. He missed the first throw, but caught the animal with his second. He led him to the gate and took an old, weather-beaten saddle blanket and bridle from the top pole of the corral. He bridled and saddled the horse expertly.

"Good-bye, Ellen," he said. He realized that he didn't want to go. Right now . . . the way she was looking at him . . .

Morgan mounted the horse quickly. He rode toward the house to get his carpetbag.

As Morgan disappeared out of the courtyard gate, Clint turned and re-entered the house. He was scowling.

For a moment Clint stood just inside the door, his scowl deepening. He didn't want Morgan to go. He had hoped . . .

He cursed softly under his breath. What had he hoped?

That Morgan would stay, of course. That Morgan would now, at last, be a son to him. That they could be close, the way a father and son were supposed to be.

He was soft in the head if he had thought that, because it wasn't possible. There was only hatred here on Sombrero any more.

The best solution, he supposed, was to forget Morgan. The best solution was to get his mind on something else. Like Luke Parfet, for instance.

The scowl faded. His eyes narrowed slightly. Suddenly he yelled, "Luis!"

A young Mexican boy came hurrying from the

direction of the kitchen. "Find Kehoe," Clint said. "Tell him I want him. *Pronto!*"

The boy scurried away. Clint began to pace back and forth up and down the length of the living room. He stopped once or twice to stare out of the window. He saw Morgan re-enter the courtyard and ride to Kehoe Lamb's quarters. After a while he saw Morgan ride out again.

He frowned helplessly. Mary was down there weeping her heart out, he supposed. And there was nothing he could do to help.

A man built an empire out of nothing. He amassed wealth until even he didn't know exactly how much he had. And he was helpless to comfort the one person in all the world he loved the most.

Almost an hour after he had sent Luis for Kehoe, he saw his foreman ride into the courtyard. Kehoe was still drunk, but he was also sick. He slid from his horse and came in the door.

"You're a hell of a lookin' sight," Clint said.

Kehoe glared at him. Clint said harshly, "Parfet will stop him before he gets to town."

Kehoe shrugged.

"Hate me if you want," Clint said. "Hate Mary too, if that's what you have to do. But the boy's got nothing to do with it."

Kehoe's voice was sullen. "What did you send that kid after me for?"

"I think it might be a good time to let Luke

44

Parfet know I won't stand for having that road closed to us. Find a dozen men. Follow Morgan. When Parfet jumps him, ride in and scare them off. Parfet won't have more'n two or three."

"What if Parfet puts up a fight?"

"He won't."

Kehoe shrugged. He stared at Clint for a moment. "Someday I'm going to kill you. You know that, don't you?"

"Anytime you're ready. In the meantime, go do what I told you to do."

Kehoe stared at him an instant more. Then he turned and went out the door. Clint heard him ride away.

He resumed his pacing. He felt helpless and inadequate, and that angered him. And he felt, for the first time in his life, uneasy and worried as though he sensed that something was going to happen over which he would have no control.

He thought of Mary, alone, weeping. He hadn't wanted to hurt her. He had never wanted that. But it seemed that everything he did . . .

If it weren't for Kehoe . . . He wished suddenly that Kehoe were dead. Maybe if Parfet did put up a scrap . . . But hell, Parfet had more sense than that.

Was that why he had sent Kehoe instead of going himself? Had he sunk to the point where . . . ? He shook his head impatiently. He began to curse, softly, savagely to himself. At last, unable to stand it any longer, he strode out, caught himself a horse, saddled and rode away toward the north.

Seeing Jane might help. Sometimes it did. But Clint couldn't hide in a bottle the way Kehoe could. The stuff only made him sick.

# 5

Mary Lamb saw Clint ride away. She saw the direction in which he rode, and knew his destination. He was going to see Jane Redd, who lived alone a dozen miles north of Sombrero headquarters in a small adobe house Clint had given her. Jane had been Luke Parfet's woman before she became Clint's. That was why Parfet hated Clint so savagely.

Her eyes were red from weeping and her face was very pale. She re-entered her house and stood for a moment with her back to the door, trying to control her trembling.

The same premonition that had touched Clint suddenly touched her as well. Something was going to happen here . . .

She shook her head almost impatiently. They had all lived under this threat of violence for years. Kehoe was like a keg of powder threatening to explode at any time.

If she'd done differently . . . She realized

46

suddenly and for the first time that her penance had been as much for the purpose of easing her own guilt as anything else. Without realizing it, she had been thinking of herself. She had let Kehoe hurt her, taking satisfaction from the pain. But in so doing, she had destroyed not only her own life but Clint's and Kehoe's and Morgan's too.

And it was too late now—to change—to repair the damage that had been done. Morgan was gone. There remained only the violence between Kehoe and Clint—the violence Kehoe had been threatening all these many years.

Who would lie dead when it was over? She could not imagine Clint Morgan dead. But she knew Kehoe, his determination, his ruthlessness . . . She began to tremble again, violently. She raised her eyes and began to pray soundlessly, more humbly than she ever had before.

Morgan rode unhurriedly, occasionally shifting position to ease one or another of the hurts he had sustained in the ruckus with Parfet. He was sorry to be leaving, but he knew he had no other choice.

He had admired and liked his mother. He had felt grudging admiration and respect for Clint. And he had been enormously attracted to Ellen Candelario. But Kehoe Lamb had made and would continue to make his staying unbearable.

He tried putting himself in Kehoe's place, tried imagining how he would feel in such a position. Much as Kehoe had felt twenty years ago, he supposed. Almost any man would feel that way.

He would be infuriated because, while he was away fighting a war, his wife and employer had betrayed him . . .

But would every man's solution be the same as Kehoe's? Would they simply banish the child and continue living with the wife, working for the employer? Would other men remain, torturing themselves as they tortured the pair who had betrayed them?

Morgan ultimately decided that he would never react as Kehoe had. If he loved the woman—if he wanted her in spite of what she'd done—he'd take her away where what had happened could be forgotten. If he wanted revenge above all else—then he'd probably kill both of them immediately. But he wouldn't drag it out for twenty years.

Kehoe must be sick, he thought. He shook himself almost visibly. He'd just as well stop thinking about it. He was leaving and it was no longer his concern.

He reached Juan Candelario's place in mid-afternoon, stopped only long enough to say hello, then continued his plodding way toward town. Fortunately, he needed to depend on Clint Morgan only for transportation to town. He had enough money of his own to take him wherever he wanted to go, to keep him until he could get a job.

The hours passed slowly. The sun settled toward the western horizon.

Morgan did not even think about Luke Parfet until he saw the man coming toward him along the narrow road, accompanied by three of his men.

Morgan stopped immediately. A frown touched his broad forehead. He didn't want trouble with Parfet now, when he was leaving anyway.

He was faced with a choice—try to outrun them or try and bluff his way through.

Neither alternative offered much chance of success. Parfet and his men were between Morgan and town so unless he turned back he had practically no chance of outrunning them.

Nor did he think Parfet was going to let him bluff his way through. He'd beaten the man pretty thoroughly before Parfet's rider intervened, roped him and dragged him off. Parfet would want to regain the face he'd lost in that episode.

For the first time in his life, Morgan wished he had a gun. But he didn't and he'd have to do the best he could.

The thought of going back now was intolerable to him. Going back would be an admission that he was unable to get across Parfet's land on his own. The only other alternative was to retreat far enough to get off Parfet's land, or lose the man, and then try and reach town by another route.

He shook his head. He didn't know this country and he was still more than fifty miles from town. He would almost certainly get lost.

Anger began to rise in him. It suddenly seemed that he'd been thrust into one impossible situation after another ever since his arrival here. And it was time it stopped.

He touched heels to his horse's sides and the animal broke into a trot. Parfet and his men halted suddenly.

Morgan grinned faintly. It surprised them, no doubt, that he didn't run. But as he approached, his chest felt tight and he had to clamp his knees hard against the horse's sides to keep them from trembling.

He didn't stop until they forced him to. He stared at Parfet, noticing with satisfaction the marks his fists had put on Parfet's face.

Parfet asked harshly, "What's the matter, did Clint run his bastard son off the place?"

He might have known this would be the pattern. It had been the pattern before and there was no reason to expect a change. He clenched his jaws against his rising anger. "If you've got a quarrel with Clint Morgan, find Clint and quarrel with him. Or haven't you got enough backbone for that?"

"You damn young pup . . ." Parfet forced his

horse ahead, alongside Morgan's animal. He reached out . . .

Morgan caught his wrist, at the same time digging his heels into his horse's sides. The animal plunged away, with Morgan dragging Parfet out of the saddle by one arm.

But Parfet could reach his gun, and did. He yanked it out, jammed the muzzle against the neck of Morgan's horse and pulled the trigger.

Morgan's horse collapsed forward, throwing him clear. Partially pinned by the horse's body, Parfet yelled, "Get the son-of-a-bitch! Get the son-of-a-bitch!"

Unhurt, Morgan came to his feet. He was going to take a beating now. But he was damned if it was going to be easy for them . . .

Parfet cursed steadily as he tried to pull his leg from beneath the horse. Parfet's riders dismounted and moved in from three sides . . .

The fist of one slammed into Morgan's right ear, knocking him against a second. He grappled with the man and flung him staggering against the one who had landed the first blow. The third swung hard . . .

Morgan ducked the swing and brought a fist up from close to the ground. It struck the man's breastbone and drove the air from him in a coughing gust. The man went back, sat down, gagging and fighting for breath.

The other two hit Morgan from behind. A blow

on the back of the neck nearly paralyzed him. Stunned, he turned and tried to fight.

But it was no use. The pair bore in, pounding him methodically, beating him back, and down, and kicking him savagely when he was.

He tried to roll away from the kicks, without success. He felt consciousness slipping away . . .

His ear, against the ground, heard the thunder of approaching hoofs. He tried to see, but his eyes and mouth were full of dirt.

A volley of shots racketed. The kicking stopped. Morgan got his eyes open long enough to see a horseman looming above him . . .

The face was unmistakable. It was the face of Kehoe Lamb. Kehoe's voice said, "Don't try to close this road again, Luke. Don't interfere with Sombrero using it. Because next time it'll be you that's dead."

The drum of hoofs again. The brief choking smell of dust in the air. Then silence, even from Luke Parfet still pinned helplessly by the horse.

Morgan rubbed his eyes with his knuckles until he could see. He sat up and looked around.

Four horses grazed forty or fifty yards away. Parfet had stopped trying to free himself and was staring at Morgan with shocked and unbelieving eyes. The three men who had been with him lay in sprawled and unnatural positions not far away.

Morgan stumbled to the horse pinning Parfet down. Dumbly, without speaking, he knelt, got hold of the horse's hind leg and heaved with all his strength.

Parfet scrambled out from under. He got to his feet. He seemed to be in a daze. He walked to one after another of his men, satisfied himself they were dead, then turned accusing eyes toward Morgan.

That accusing look was a release for Morgan's fury. He strode to Parfet and slapped the side of his face so hard the man's head rocked violently with the blow. Morgan yelled, "You dumb son-of-a-bitch! You stupid fool! Didn't you know something like this would happen if you kept pulling Clint Morgan's tail? Did you think he was going to let you get away with it?"

Parfet stared at him with eyes that seemed glazed with shock. "They're dead. They're all three dead!"

"You're lucky you're not!" Suddenly Morgan's anger was gone. He felt a little sick. He was beginning to see what the inevitable consequences of this must be. Even in New Mexico you couldn't kill three men and get away with it. Not even if your name was Clint Morgan and you owned half a county.

"What do you want to do?" he said. "I'll help you do whatever you want to do."

"I got to get them home. I got to bury 'em." Plainly Parfet still wasn't thinking clearly.

But when he'd had time . . . when the shock

53

had worn away . . . he'd hightail it for town and swear out arrest warrants. For Kehoe. For Clint. For whoever else he had recognized.

"All right then," Morgan said. "Let's load them up."

Between them, they lifted one after another of the dead men to their saddles and tied them face downward so that they would not slip off. Morgan had never seen a dead man before, except for his uncle and he had been lying peacefully in a casket at the undertaker's in Illinois. This was different. These men had died violently, all in the space of a minute or two. There was blood . . . on their clothes . . . One of them had a bluish hole in his forehead from which blood oozed . . .

Morgan turned his back to Parfet, feeling sick. But he didn't vomit. He just felt like it.

Parfet, seeming to understand that Morgan would have to have a horse, mounted awkwardly behind one of the bodies. Morgan handed him the reins of the other two horses and Parfet, without speaking again, rode away.

Morgan watched him a moment. Closing this road to Clint had been an act of bluff, from which Parfet had never really expected this kind of violence.

He turned, untied his carpetbag from the saddle of the downed horse, then retied it to the saddle of the remaining horse. He mounted and turned toward town.

He couldn't leave now, he realized. He was a material witness at the very least and the sheriff wouldn't let him leave.

He realized something else. Clint Morgan's power here was about to be put to the test.

# 6

There was utter silence among the men of Sombrero as Kehoe Lamb led them away from the scene of sudden death. Kehoe rode in the lead, spurring savagely, as though by running he could outrun the consequences of what he had done.

He felt as he once had felt as a small boy when, in a fit of sudden rage, he had smashed his favorite toy. Right now he couldn't even remember what the toy had been but he did remember the awful feeling of having done something he bitterly regretted, something that could never be undone.

Three men were dead back there. And why? He tried to tell himself it was Clint Morgan's fault. Clint had, after all, given him orders to follow Morgan and see that he got through all right.

But in his innermost self, Kehoe understood that Clint had not been ordering murder. Clint had felt that a show of force was all that was necessary.

The trouble was . . . He had deliberately let it go too far. He had waited, vengefully, so that Morgan would be thoroughly beaten before he intervened.

He began to curse, softly, beneath his breath. His face was a ghastly shade of gray. For the first time in his life, Kehoe Lamb was scared clear through.

He could almost visualize himself mounting a scaffold's steps. He could almost feel the noose against his neck.

Involuntarily he raised a hand and ran it beneath his collar. Damn! Damn! Damn!

Gradually, the mechanisms of self-justification began to work in his mind as he desperately sought a way out. Clint was the one who would mount the scaffold. And the men who had actually done the killing. But how would anyone know precisely who they were? They sure as hell weren't going to admit anything. Even Kehoe wasn't prepared to admit he had fired the first shot.

No. However he tried to excuse himself, however he tried to shift the blame, he knew well enough who would be held responsible.

He slowed his horse. He needed time to think before he faced Clint Morgan with this news.

The men ranged up alongside of him. Phil Dexter, one of the older hands, asked, "What the hell got into you, Kehoe? Why'd you hold us back so long? You knew they was goin' to jump that kid. If we'd rode in there right away . . . We'd have got there before they killed Morgan's horse and they wouldn't have gone for their guns."

Kehoe turned his head and stared at him. Phil was about sixty and his face was like a relief map of New Mexico. He was the ugliest man Kehoe had ever known but his eyes, deep in their sockets, were calm and steadily reproachful.

Kehoe said irritably, "If the bunch of you hadn't been so goddam trigger happy . . ."

"They followed your lead, that's all," Phil said. "You shot first."

Kehoe said sharply, "Shut up! What's done is done. Clint gave the order anyway. Let him worry about it."

Phil let his horse fall back with a faint shrug. The rest of the men fell back with him and Kehoe could hear them talking among themselves. He couldn't make out their words but he knew well enough what they were talking about.

Maybe Clint's power and influence could get the thing hushed up. The only trouble was . . . a lot of people in the county hated Clint. And while Parfet wasn't overly well liked, he would become a symbol to them now. A symbol of Clint's highhandedness. There'd be plenty of people saying that it was time somebody took Clint Morgan down a peg.

He began to consider the fix he'd put Clint into by his actions today. Let Clint get out of this one if he could. Let Clint see if he was a big enough man to get out of this.

Morgan held the horse at a steady, bone-jolting trot for miles. Then, as much to rest himself as the horse, he let him walk a while.

For a moment he wondered if Kehoe Lamb had made the attack on his own responsibility, but he shook his head. No. Kehoe wouldn't have cared if Parfet had half-killed him. The attack had to have been Clint's idea. But why hadn't he led it himself?

There could be a number of reasons. But the one that seemed most reasonable was that Clint thought Kehoe might be killed. It was an ugly reason that reflected no credit on Clint.

Morgan couldn't guess what the exact consequences would be. Out here at least. He knew what they would have been in Illinois. Clint, Kehoe, and the men with Kehoe would have been arrested and jailed. They would have been tried, convicted, and sentenced according to their guilt. But Clint and Kehoe would have paid the heaviest penalties.

The sun set behind the western hills and the grays of dusk crept across the land. A few stars winked out.

Though there was no moon, starlight made the narrow road visible. Aching muscles and rump and thighs sore from so much unaccustomed time in the saddle, kept Morgan awake, but occasionally he did drowse. During one of these drowsing periods his horse entered the sleeping town.

One light only was visible to him and he headed for it automatically, not knowing where else to go. It turned out to be in the railroad station.

He swung from his horse, tied the animal to a post and went inside. A telegraph key clacked monotonously. The man operating it turned his head as Morgan came in.

He was middle-aged, gray, and tired of eye and face. He wore a green eyeshade against the glare of the lamp hanging overhead. "Where's the sheriff's office?" Morgan asked.

The man gave him directions, staring at him curiously as he did. As Morgan turned, the man opened his mouth as though to speak, then closed it without doing so.

Morgan realized that he had noted his resemblance to Clint. With a light shrug, he remounted his horse, then rode on into the darkened town.

He found the sheriff's office without difficulty. It was a square, stone building, standing out even in darkness among the adobe buildings that surrounded it. The windows, even in front, were barred.

Morgan dismounted, tied his horse, then pounded on the door. Nothing stirred inside, so he kicked it with his toe.

"All right. All right! Don't kick the damned thing down!" The words were followed by a stream of Spanish, which, Morgan supposed, was repetition in case the sheriff's caller turned out to be Mexican.

He heard the bar drawn back, heard a metal bolt, and the door swung open. Into the pitch-black opening he said, "I'm Morgan Lamb. I want to talk to you."

"All right. Come on in. I'll light the lamp."

Morgan waited until a match flared, then went inside. The man, who wore only red-flannel underwear, lighted the lamp and lowered the chimney. He turned, his hair mussed, the marks of sleep plain in his eyes and face.

He crossed the room, took his pants from the back of a chair and put them on. He sat down on the edge of the rumpled cot and pulled on his boots. He reached for a long black Mexican cigar and lighted it at the top of the lamp chimney. He blew a cloud of smoke at Morgan and said, "Well?"

He reminded Morgan of Juan Candelario, except that he was not so grossly fat. He also bore a resemblance to Pete. "I'm Pete's brother, if that's what you're thinking," he said slowly. "I'm Jaime Candelario. Everybody calls me Jimmy. I'm the sheriff."

Morgan wondered suddenly if Pete Candelario had been with Kehoe Lamb—if he had participated in the attack. He hadn't seen Pete, but that didn't mean he hadn't been there.

"You'll get this from Mr. Parfet as soon as he can get here, so it seemed like a good idea for me to tell you first," Morgan said.

"Ruckus out there? Luke try to close Clint's road?"

Morgan nodded. "He stopped me on the way to town. There was some trouble and he shot my horse. Kehoe Lamb and some other men arrived. There was some shooting. Three of Parfet's men are dead."

The sheriff released a stream of Spanish invective. His voice was hushed and shocked. Then he said, in English, "That does it! That goddam Parfet shoulda known he couldn't pull Clint's tail. I told him. I told him a dozen times if I told him once."

"What will happen?"

Jaime Candelario spread his hands helplessly, puffing furiously on the cigar. "Anything. Everything. The whole damn county could blow sky high."

"What will you do?"

"Nothin', until Luke comes in to swear the warrants out. Then I guess I'll serve 'em. That's what I'm paid to do."

Morgan turned toward the door. "Is there a hotel in town?"

"Yeah, but you'll pay hell gettin' a room now.

61

The clerk goes to bed at midnight. Take that cot over there. It's my deputy's, but he won't be back tonight."

Morgan nodded. All the sleeplessness, all the exertion and pounding he had endured suddenly were overwhelming to him. He sat down on the cot and took off his boots. He laid back for a moment . . .

He was almost instantly asleep.

When he awakened, there was daylight in the room. But it was a cheerless light, either of early dawn, or that of a cloudy day.

He got up, staggered to the barred window and looked outside. It was raining hard. The street was a sea of mud. Jaime Candelario was standing in front of the building, wearing a yellow poncho and a battered tan hat.

And there were horsemen. Three of them. And three led horses. The saddles of two held a single face-down body each. The third had two bodies tied across its back.

Morgan frowned. He recognized the three led horses. They were the three upon which he and Luke Parfet had loaded the bodies of Parfet's men yesterday. He recognized the bodies too, though they were stiff now. But the fourth body . . .

Horror touched him with the recognition of it. It was Luke Parfet who laid dead across the rump of the third horse. Luke Parfet, whom Morgan had last seen riding away toward home leading two of the horses behind.

Jaime spoke to the three men and waved an arm downstreet. They rode away, leading the horses with their grisly burdens behind.

Jaime turned. His face was strained. His eyes met Morgan's through the barred window.

Morgan felt a touch of fear, a cold tingling along his spine. He realized that both the sheriff and the men who had brought the bodies in thought he had killed Parfet.

It shouldn't be hard to prove he hadn't, he thought. Out where the battle had occurred there were tracks. It should be plain enough to anyone that Parfet had ridden away and that Morgan had continued on toward town.

He stared at the muddy street, in which growing puddles lay. It must have been raining a good part of the night . . . It must have begun not long after he went to sleep . . .

What tracks were left out there would be gone. Or so badly blurred they wouldn't prove anything.

Panic touched him briefly. He crossed to the gunrack against the wall and took a rifle down. He swung around as the door opened.

"You think I killed Parfet, don't you?" Morgan said.

Jaime nodded. "Put the gun down. It won't do you a damn bit of good. You may look like Clint, but that's as far as it goes. Parfet was shot in the back."

"Why would I shoot him? Why?"

"He and his men beat the hell out of you twice. That's reason enough." Candelario's eyes were hard, like tiny bits of stone in his ordinarily pleasant, moon-shaped face.

Morgan raised the gun. He worked the lever, not sure it was loaded until a live cartridge clattered on the floor. "You and me are going to walk down to the stable," he said. "You're going to get a fresh horse for me. Turn around."

Candelario hesitated. There were things in his face Morgan didn't understand. Reluctantly, he turned around.

Morgan snatched his gun from its holster and stuffed it into his belt. Uneasily certain in his own mind that Jaime Candelario could have shot him with ease, he followed the sheriff out the door into the pouring rain.

# 7

It was only a short walk from the sheriff's office to the stable, standing tall at the edge of town. Morgan stayed a step behind Candelario, carrying the rifle so that it pointed at the ground. He saw only one person, a woman, hurrying along, head down in the rain.

Reaching the stable, they went inside, into the warm, dry air that smelled of manure, and horses, and dusty hay and grain. A man shuffled toward them, laying his pitchfork aside as he did. "Get me a horse, Felipe," the sheriff said.

"For you, señor?"

"No. But get a good horse anyway."

"*Si.*" The man shuffled back in the direction he had come. After a short time he returned, leading a tall, gleaming black. "Saddle him, Felipe," Jaime said.

The man led the horse to the tackroom and went inside for a saddle. "You're making a mistake," Candelario said. "You don't know the country. And I'll have to come after you."

Morgan felt a slow-smoldering anger. He had been dragged on the end of a rope before he'd been here twelve hours. He'd been insulted and cursed and beaten a second time. Now he was accused of a murder.

Worst of all, he had an uneasy feeling that if he did let himself be brought to trial it wouldn't be Morgan Lamb that was on trial at all. It would be Clint Morgan. And Sombrero. And Kehoe Lamb.

Yet he knew the sheriff was right. He didn't know the country. He had no friends. He was unfamiliar with guns, upon which he now must depend for the defense of his life.

He was also Clint Morgan's son regardless of the circumstances connected with his birth. He

65

had inherited Clint Morgan's looks. Perhaps he had also inherited from Clint the other qualities that had made it possible for him to acquire Sombrero and hold it all these years against those who would take it away from him.

Felipe brought the horse, looking puzzledly from the sheriff to Morgan and back. Morgan mounted the horse, but held him there for a moment until Felipe had shuffled away. Then he glanced down and said, "I didn't kill Parfet, Sheriff, whether you believe it or not. I don't want to kill anyone, but I'm not going to trial here where any jury you pick will be taking out on me their hate for Clint. I'll shoot if you come after me."

Candelario shrugged fatalistically. Morgan turned the horse and rode out into the rain.

He dug heels into the spirited animal's sides immediately and the black broke into a run. He raced recklessly out of town, pointed north.

Morgan didn't know where he was going to go. He had no food, no blankets, not even a slicker to keep him dry. But if he put enough distance between himself and the town before Candelario rode in pursuit, perhaps the rain would hide his trail. He could only hope it would.

There was a man somewhere who had shot Luke Parfet in the back. Impossible as it seemed right now, Morgan had to find that man. Or get clear out of the country for good. Or stand trial for something he hadn't done in a community almost certain to convict him simply because he was Clint Morgan's son.

The choices weren't too good. But anger kept him from dwelling on the fact. He ran the horse steadily until the animal was ready to stop.

The sheriff watched Morgan ride away from the stable entrance. His face was impassive, but his eyes were troubled. After several moments he went out again into the rain and trudged back to his office through the mud.

He wasn't worried about Morgan getting away. He was more concerned that Morgan would get himself shot before he caught up with him.

But Morgan wasn't his biggest problem. His biggest problem was Clint.

He was sitting behind his desk when the door opened and the three who had brought in the bodies of Parfet and his men entered.

Their boots were muddy and they stopped just inside the door to stamp it off. All wore slickers, and the faces of all three were angry. One, the tallest, said, "You got him locked up, Jaime?"

"He pulled a gun on me," Candelario said. "He got away."

"Got away?" The man's voice was incredulous.

Candelario shrugged. "I could have shot him." He stared placidly at the tall man, Nate Duffy, who was Parfet's neighbor on the south.

"Why the hell didn't you?"

The sheriff asked patiently, "Are you trying to start a range war, Nate? You want Clint Morgan on your tail? Then you go shoot him. And see what happens to you when Clint hears about it."

"You can't just . . . !"

"Let him get away with it? Nobody's going to get away with anything. I'll go out and see Clint today. Whoever cut Parfet down will go to trial."

"Whaddaya mean, whoever cut Parfet down. We know. We know who killed them three men of his too."

Candelario stooped and dug in a bottom drawer of his desk. He came up with several sheets of paper. "Name names and sign these warrants and I'll serve 'em."

The tall man's face showed hesitation briefly. He turned his head and looked at his companions. When he turned back to Candelario his face was set. "All right, by God, I will. I'll name Clint and Kehoe and that kid that just got away from you. You bring 'em in and we'll find out just how big Clint Morgan is."

The sheriff began to write. When he had finished, he shoved the papers across the littered desk at Duffy. "Sign 'em."

Duffy did. Candelario got up. The thing was started. He knew that before it was finished, more men would be dead. But he had no choice. He couldn't ignore the fact that four men had been killed.

Yet he knew as well that the motives behind Duffy's wrath had little to do with the murders of Parfet and his men. He knew how many others, besides Duffy, coveted Sombrero range. Sombrero was ringed with them.

Every one of them knew that all they had to do was get Clint Morgan out of the way. Then they could move in.

Clint had been stupid to give them this chance to get him out of the way. Unless Clint hadn't had anything to do with it . . .

The door closed behind Duffy. Candelario got up and put his slicker on. His face was suddenly more worried than it yet had been.

If Clint hadn't been involved . . . Morgan was the only one who knew it, except for the men who had been there. If Morgan was dead no one could prove Clint hadn't been responsible.

Morgan, therefore, was in considerable danger, not all of it from the law. But perhaps it wouldn't occur to Sombrero's enemies that Morgan could prove Clint had not been present at the time of the killings. Perhaps they were too sure Clint *had* been there.

In his own mind, however, Jaime was fairly certain that Clint had not. In the first place, Clint would not have delayed. He would not have held back until Morgan had been beaten up.

Furthermore, although Clint was tough and had dealt summarily once or twice in the past with rustlers or horse thieves, he had more sense than to cold-bloodedly murder Parfet's three men and then leave Parfet alive to testify against him. And he had more decency than to kill Parfet by shooting him in the back afterward simply because he was a witness.

Another thought occurred to Jaime as he went out the door. If Kehoe was the one responsible, and if Kehoe had killed Parfet to shut him up, then he might also kill Morgan for the same reason. He might, in fact, relish killing Morgan because Morgan was a constant reminder of his wife's infidelity.

The sheriff walked heavily to the stable. "Felipe, get my horse for me."

He watched absently as Felipe followed his orders. He mounted the saddled horse and rode out into the rain. He lifted his face to the sky and mildly cursed the rain for destroying tracks the way it had. He pointed the horse northward out of town, following Morgan's rapidly dimming trail because it happened to be going the same way.

He felt brief pity for Morgan. It had been rough for him, coming home this way—to find out that he was not Kehoe's son but Clint's instead—to be beaten and dragged and forced to leave because his presence made things intolerable for everyone at Sombrero, including himself.

And yet—talking to Morgan last night and again this morning—he had seen in the young man something of the strength he saw in Clint.

He nodded almost with satisfaction when Morgan's trail veered away from its straight northerly course and turned west. Morgan wasn't going home, then. He wasn't going to run to Clint. He intended to work his troubles out in his own way.

Jaime silently wished him luck. Then he relaxed himself in the saddle against the long, cold ride to Sombrero headquarters almost a hundred miles away.

Morgan rode steadily north for a long while before he turned aside, trying to reach some decision as to where he could go. He didn't want to leave the country for he sensed he would be hunted the rest of his days if he did.

Going back to Sombrero, running to Clint, was equally intolerable. Yet for a long time he could think of no place else to go.

His mind wandered aimlessly. He remembered Pete, and Juan Candelario. And Ellen . . .

Ellen lived on Sombrero, but Juan did not. Perhaps he could get food and blankets from Juan. If he beat the sheriff to Juan's place.

Abruptly he turned his horse west, kicking him

into a slow lope as he did. He rode west about a mile, then turned north again, paralleling the narrow road.

With his course decided, he pushed the horse as hard as he dared. The miles dropped behind rapidly.

Toward noon, the clouds began to thin and shortly thereafter the rain slackened and stopped. Morgan was wet to the skin. He was shivering almost uncontrollably. He doubted if he ever felt anything as pleasant as the sun, coming out and shining warmly on his chilled body.

The land began to steam. The neck of Morgan's horse steamed and so did his clothes. His shivering gradually stopped.

He reached Candelario's place in midafternoon, stopped in sight of it long enough to ascertain that no saddled horses were tied down there. To be doubly sure, he rode down to the road and examined it for tracks. There were none.

Reassured, he rode in and dismounted at Juan Candelario's door. But it was not Juan who came to the door. It was Ellen.

Morgan swung stiffly from his horse. "Is Juan here?"

She shook her head, eyes studying him disconcertingly. "He and Maria went to Mr. Parfet's place to see if they could help. They won't be back until late tonight."

He hesitated uncertainly. "I was going to ask . . . if I could get some food and blankets . . ." He stopped.

"Is something the matter? I thought you went to town."

"I did . . ." He stared at her, wondering how much he ought to say. At last he said, "I'm accused of shooting Parfet in the back. I'm on the run."

"You? Where can you run? You don't even know the country. First thing you'll do is get lost."

He grinned. "That's what I want to do right now. Get so lost nobody can find me."

"What about Clint? He . . ." She stopped and shook her head. "No. I can see why you can't go there." She frowned a moment, then said decisively, "Well, don't just stand there. Come in and dry yourself out while I put some things in a sack and leave a note for Juan."

"Note? Why a note?"

"Because I'm going with you, that's why. You haven't got a chance unless I do."

"What about your uncle . . . the sheriff? He's the one that's hunting me."

She tossed her head impatiently. "I doubt if he's hunting very hard. Or he'd have caught you before you got this far."

He sank into a chair and stared at her back as she worked. He noticed the flush that crept into

73

her cheeks and darkened the back of her neck.

Again he felt the strong pull of attraction and suddenly he was glad he hadn't left the country instead of coming here.

# 8

Jaime Candelario was not surprised when, half a mile short of his brother Juan's house, he cut the trail of Morgan Lamb, entering the road. Morgan had had to go someplace for food, he realized. And this was the most logical of places since it was one of the only two places with which Morgan was familiar He knew Pete would have stopped at Juan's on his way to Sombrero after picking Morgan up at the train.

He rode in a bit warily. He doubted if Morgan was a killer, doubted too if he had killed Luke Parfet. But Morgan had been pushed considerably since arriving here. Maybe he had been pushed too far.

No shots greeted him, however, from the house. He dismounted before the door and went inside.

The place was empty. But to Jaime's keen glance, the preparations that had been made to supply Morgan with food were apparent. He cursed softly when he realized that Ellen must have accompanied the fugitive.

Her presence with Morgan would make him

hard to catch. There were few men hereabouts who knew the country better than Ellen did. And when she had been small, Jaime himself had taught her most of what he knew about hiding trail.

Yet her presence with Morgan was not without its advantages. Morgan would be safer with her than with anybody else. He would stay alive, at least, until Jaime got around to him.

He fixed himself a meal almost absently, frowning occasionally at his thoughts. He didn't like what was ahead. He didn't like arresting Clint Morgan, because he understood what would happen when he did.

He liked Clint. He was probably one of the few in Santiago County who did. He understood Clint, perhaps because his brother Pete worked for him, perhaps because his brother Juan lived out here on the edge of Sombrero range. Or perhaps it was because he had grown up here, and as a boy had known Clint fairly well.

Clint was hated. That was indisputable. But he had not earned all the hatred given him by the people who lived on the edges of Sombrero range.

Clint had come here nearly thirty years ago— when the land belonged to the wild tribes, when there was no law closer than Santa Fe. He had risked his life half a hundred times to build Sombrero into what it was. He had claimed and

75

taken land no one else wanted because they were afraid of the Comanche and the Kiowa.

Later, when the tribes had been subdued and driven south, when settlers came in, he had held Sombrero against them too and had refused to give up a single square inch of it. Since he held most of the grass that amounted to anything for over two hundred miles, they resented him bitterly for it.

They resented the fact that grass went to waste on Sombrero while on their own ranches it was eaten down almost to the ground. They resented Sombrero riders, who drove their hungry cattle back.

And there were other things . . . Jaime remembered once, when two of Sombrero's neighbors drove off a dozen Sombrero horses. Clint caught up with them . . .

Jaime finished eating and rolled a wheat-straw cigarette. He puffed nervously, still frowning faintly. Perhaps Clint wouldn't have been so harsh if the pair hadn't practically spit in his eye. But they had and had cursed him, and he ended up hanging them both from an ancient piñon limb.

Another time . . . when another of Sombrero's neighbors tried to repair his failure to make a living on his own land by stealing Clint Morgan's beef . . . Clint caught up with him and with the two he'd thrown in with. They decided to fight and it ended with one of them dead and another permanently crippled by a bullet in the knee.

All of this had little bearing on what he had to do, Jaime thought. He was still Sheriff of Santiago County. He had warrants for Clint, for Kehoe, and for Morgan Lamb. He had to serve them or resign.

The consequences . . . well, Clint should have thought of the consequences before he sent Kehoe and a dozen men to jump Parfet and his men. Clint should have known that this was different than hanging horse thieves or shooting rustlers to get his cattle back. Parfet had been on his own land. He might have been wrong in closing the road but the right or wrong of that should have been settled in the courts.

Now . . . if Clint and Kehoe went to jail . . . there would be no one at Sombrero capable of holding it. Those surrounding it would gobble it up, clear to the boundaries of the original Spanish grant. Someone might even show up who could throw a cloud on Clint's title to the Spanish grant. It was happening all over New Mexico and Jaime suspected that someone up in Santa Fe was doing some mighty clever forgeries.

He shrugged resignedly, got up and went outside. He'd just as well get on with it. He was only the sheriff and sworn to do a certain job. If

Clint paid too heavily for what had been done . . . there wasn't anything Jaime could do about it. It would just have to be.

Clint Morgan sat broodingly in one of the huge, rawhide-covered chairs staring emptily at nothing. Occasionally a frown would touch his craggy face, and sometimes it would soften briefly with some small memory.

He was thinking, remembering the past. He was regretting, too, and wondering if he could have done anything to prevent things coming to this final bitterness. Morgan was gone and would never return. Kehoe's hatred had so warped and twisted him that he wasn't even the same man he had been twenty years ago. All that remained . . . Kehoe would ultimately go beyond the point of self-control . . . soon perhaps. Then either Kehoe or Clint would die, and Mary would leave Sombrero, never to return.

Oddly, even now Clint could not regret what had happened between Mary and himself so long ago. Out of it had come nothing but hatred and bitterness. But it was one of the sweetest memories he had.

And Morgan . . . Clint's face softened momentarily. Morgan had been raised well by Mary's brother and his wife. He would be a fine man. He already was, in spite of his lack of age and experience.

Clint wondered where he would now go and what he would do. There had been a time when he dreamed sometimes of Morgan coming here and taking over the running of Sombrero ranch. It would all belong to Morgan some day anyway. Clint had no one else to leave it to.

But Morgan wouldn't . . . he couldn't love the land the way Clint did. This land now held nothing but unpleasant memories for him.

Perhaps in the emptiness of his personal life, Clint thought, was the explanation for his driving ambition with regard to Sombrero, to this land. And yet it had not all been emptiness. He remembered Morgan as a baby, toddling along the gallery outside that door. He remembered the few times he had held Morgan in his arms . . .

Nor had the later years been all emptiness. The high points of his days had been glimpses of Mary—walking along the gallery—hanging out clothes in back—climbing into the buggy for a trip to town or to one of the neighbors for some shindig or other.

It was late . . . it was nearly morning, he thought. It would soon be getting light . . .

His thoughts were interrupted by a clatter of hoofs in the courtyard—many hoofs. He got up and walked to the window. Kehoe and the men had returned, which meant Morgan had made it safely across Luke Parfet's land.

He opened the door, carrying a lamp. He peered at the milling group.

They seemed subdued. He didn't see Kehoe anywhere . . .

"Where's Kehoe?" he asked harshly.

For a moment nobody answered him. Then Phil Dexter swung stiffly from his horse and, leading him, walked to where Clint stood. "He must've fallen behind or something. I haven't seen him for two or three hours."

"What's the matter? What happened?"

Phil scuffed the dirt with the toe of his boot. Then he looked at Clint determinedly. "It didn't turn out the way it should've, Clint. One of Parfet's men went for a gun . . ."

"For Christ's sake, what happened? Don't stand there all night beating around the bush!"

"Three of Parfet's men got killed."

For an instant Clint stood frozen. Then he looked beyond Phil at the other men. He said heavily, "Put your horses up. Go to bed."

Phil stood half a dozen feet away, waiting uneasily. Clint said, "Come on in and give me all of it."

He turned and re-entered the house, with Phil following. He put down the lamp and poured himself a drink. He poured another and handed it to Phil. "Now."

Phil gulped the raw whisky and slammed the glass down on the table angrily. "It didn't have to happen! I don't like blaming somebody else, but Kehoe held us back so's they'd have a chance to beat Morgan up before we interfered. Morgan did pretty well for himself. He yanked Luke out of his saddle, but Luke shot his horse. Maybe that was why they went for their guns. Maybe they remembered what happened to Nate Carmichael a couple of years ago when he stole those horses from you."

Clint said, almost wearily, "Go on."

"When they went for their guns . . . well hell, we opened up. I think Kehoe shot first, but I couldn't swear to it. You know how those things are. Somebody starts shooting and the first thing you know everybody's shooting. Anyhow, when it was over, all three of Parfet's men were dead."

"How about Parfet?"

"He was pinned down by Morgan's horse and didn't have a gun. He was still pinned down when we left. I suppose Morgan got him loose."

Clint felt a smoldering anger he found difficult to control. "All right, Phil," he said. "Go to bed."

Phil got up, glanced at the whisky bottle and then at Clint. "There'll be trouble over this," he said. "It ain't like hanging horse thieves or shooting rustlers. Parfet was on his own land."

Clint said impatiently, "All right, Phil."

"Reckon I could have another . . . ?"

"Damn it, take the bottle! But get out of here!"

Phil snatched the bottle and hurried to the

door. He went out, closing it behind him with exaggerated quietness.

Clint began to pace angrily back and forth across the room. He understood what had happened all right. Kehoe had wanted to see Morgan beaten half to death. And that's what Parfet would have done to him too. In fact it was probably what had happened in spite of Phil's statement that Morgan had done all right. He wished suddenly that he'd asked Phil how badly Morgan had been beaten before Kehoe interfered.

Part of it, though, was his own damn fault. It was he that Parfet hated. He cursed ruefully to himself because it was ironic in a way. Kehoe hated him because of Mary. And Parfet hated him because of a woman too. Because of Jane Redd.

He supposed Parfet had loved her, though he took a damn poor way of showing it. He'd mistreated her and had even occasionally beaten her. And when his wife found out he was seeing her . . .

That had been when Clint stepped in. Jane had been afraid for her life and had come to Sombrero for help . . .

He wasn't very proud of what happened afterward. He'd offered her that adobe house north of here. But he hadn't really meant to . . . afterward . . .

He kicked out angrily at a chair. It clattered as it crashed against the wall. The trouble had been

. . . Jane was attractive . . . She had been willing. After all, she'd been both desperate and afraid. And Clint had been . . . well hell, he was a man. A man with a man's needs. And he had taken good care of Jane. Ever since he'd started seeing her.

He didn't know whether Mary knew about Jane or not. He supposed she did. Kehoe wouldn't miss as good a chance as Jane provided for hurting her.

He forced his thoughts away from Jane. He forced himself to think of what the consequences of the three killings were going to be.

Neither he nor Kehoe was going to get away with it. Jaime Candelario would be out here with warrants just as soon as Parfet could swear them out. Not only for Kehoe, either. For him too. Because he had given Kehoe the order to see that Morgan got through to town all right.

The size of Sombrero . . . his money . . . This time these things weren't going to do much good. His neighbors had tried to get him twice before—when he'd hanged those horse thieves —when he'd shot two of the rustlers. They hadn't succeeded in making it stick, but it was going to be different this time. Parfet's three men had been on Parfet's land. It was going to be obvious to anyone that Kehoe's presence there with twelve armed men wasn't an accident.

If it hadn't been for Kehoe's hatred, though . . .

If it hadn't been that Parfet hated him because of Jane . . .

But Kehoe did hate him and so did Luke. And three of Luke's men were dead because of it.

He sat down, reached absently for the bottle and found it gone. He took a black cigar out of his pocket and lighted it. If he gave himself up when Jaime Candelario came after him . . . if he allowed Jaime to take him into custody . . .

Hell, Sombrero would fall apart. They'd move in on him from all four sides. They'd leave him with nothing but the Spanish Grant, and they might even find a way of taking that. By the time he got out of jail, if he ever did, he'd be lucky if he had a horse.

He puffed on the cigar furiously. The sky outside was turning gray, he noticed, but still he did not blow out the lamp. Nor did he consider going to bed. He just sat staring emptily at nothing in particular. He'd been fighting all his life. But he knew that the fight coming up for him would be the toughest one he had ever fought.

This time he'd be fighting something that hadn't even been here when he came, something that had been getting stronger every year. He would be fighting the law itself.

# 9

There was an air of waiting about Sombrero all that day. Rumors spread among the hands, among the families of the Mexican vaqueros who lived in the village of adobe huts a quarter of a mile from the house. The rumors started small. But by the time dusk came, it was being said that the Governor in Santa Fe was sending troops—that they would arrive tomorrow or the next day—that there would be a pitched battle because old Clint Morgan never would give up.

Little work was done, because no one wanted to leave. And Clint didn't send them out. He couldn't be sure Jaime Candelario would come alone. He couldn't even be sure Jaime would come. Perhaps Parfet's friends and neighbors would take things into their own hands and come prepared to attack Sombrero and burn its buildings to the ground.

He gave the rumor of troops from Santa Fe no credence at all. Things had not progressed that far. They might, in time, but they hadn't yet.

So he paced the huge living room, scowling and occasionally cursing savagely under his breath.

Often during that endless day he wished he could talk to Mary. Once or twice he started for the door. But he always stopped. And always he turned back. There was no use in worrying her. And there was really no way that she could help. She could only reassure him and, perhaps, give him sympathy.

He couldn't help wondering where Kehoe was. He couldn't help wondering why he had not returned with the others and wondering what his absence meant. That he was up to some further deviltry, probably. Knowing Kehoe, he could hardly believe anything else.

Noon came and passed, and still Jaime did not arrive. Clint ate his dinner alone at the head of the tremendous oaken table in the dining room. Afterward, he lighted another black cigar and went out onto the gallery to pace angrily back and forth.

The air was hot and humid after the rain that had fallen the night before. No small breeze stirred. From outside the courtyard Clint could hear the sounds his men and their families made. He heard a Spanish guitar being lazily strummed. He heard a dog bark and heard someone quarreling in the adobe village beyond the wall.

Clint knew Mary was there—in her doorway, even though he didn't turn his head. He knew she was there because he felt her presence and her thoughts, because once he thought he smelled her light perfume. He clenched his hands at his sides and clamped his teeth tight against the cigar. He went back inside.

He paced back and forth, like a caged and angry lion. The minutes dragged past, dragged into hours that seemed interminable.

The clock was chiming four when he heard the beat of hoofs. He went out onto the gallery in time to see Jaime Candelario come pounding into the courtyard.

Jaime pulled his horse to a halt and sat there staring down at Clint. "Get down and come on in," Clint said.

There was strong tension in him, tension that increased with his realization that he was not, today, wearing his gun. Jaime dismounted and tied his horse, then crossed the gallery stiffly with the dry comment, "It's a damn long ride out here."

Clint didn't reply. He followed Jaime in. He found a bottle and poured the sheriff a drink and another for himself.

Jaime gulped it, coughed, and said, "Know why I'm here?"

"I know."

"Where's Kehoe?"

Clint shrugged. "I've got no idea. He didn't come in with the rest of the men."

"I've got warrants, Clint. I've got to serve 'em. One for you and one for Kehoe and one for Morgan Lamb."

"Why Morgan? What the hell did he do?"

"The warrant charges him with killing Luke. By shooting him in the back."

87

Something cold began to grow in Clint's deep chest. He hadn't known Luke was dead. Phil had said that Luke had been pinned down by Morgan's horse—that he had still been alive when they left.

"Where'd Luke get killed?" Clint asked softly. "Phil told me he was still alive when Kehoe and the rest of 'em left."

Jaime shrugged. "Somewhere between the place the three were killed and home, I guess."

"Didn't you read the tracks? I'd think . . ." He stopped suddenly, remembering how hard it had rained last night.

Jaime nodded. "The rain. They were all washed out."

The coldness in Clint's chest was spreading. It was not only he who was in danger now. It was Morgan too. Morgan would pay equally for the hatred people felt toward him and toward Kehoe. Morgan would go down with the two of them simply because he was . . . because he was who he was.

"Where's Morgan now? In jail?" Clint asked.

Candelario shook his head. "Huh-uh." He grinned at Clint uneasily. "He got away. I could've shot him I suppose, but I was damned if I was going to. He left town half an hour before I did."

"Where'd he go? Where could he go? Of all the god-dam . . ."

"Easy now. He's all right. He went to Juan's

88

place. I suppose it was Ellen who fixed him up with grub and blankets. The two of them went off together. She knows the country as well as I do, and she's smart about hiding trail. He'll be all right for now."

Clint stared steadily at him. "So you're going to get us one at a time, is that it? Me first. Then Kehoe. Then Morgan. Huh-uh. You ain't going to get me, Jaime. I'm not going. You know damned well what those buzzards will do to Sombrero if I go to jail."

"You might be able to get out on bond."

"On a murder charge? In this county? You know better than that."

His eyes watchful, Clint fumbled in his pocket for another cigar. He knew there wasn't one, but he had to get to the desk somehow. He got up, still fumbling through his pockets, and walked with an appearance of absent-mindedness, toward the desk. He reached it, reached for the drawer that held his gun . . .

Jaime's voice cracked like a whip. "Clint! Don't do it!"

"Do what?" Desperation . . . a feeling of failure was overwhelming in Clint. He'd never been able to act a part. He couldn't act one now. He hadn't fooled the sheriff a bit.

"You know what. Don't open that drawer and reach for your gun. I'll have to shoot you if you do."

Clint shrugged. For an instant he stood there frozen. He was damned if Jaime was going to take him in. It was the end of everything if he did. Just as well make a try for the gun. Just as well take the chance . . .

He heard the faintest of sounds in the direction of the door. Jaime heard it too, but he didn't turn his head. A slight grin of relief touched Clint's wide mouth.

"You lose, Jaime," he said. "Phil's standing behind you with a shotgun."

"It won't work, Clint."

"See for yourself."

"And give you a chance to grab the gun in that drawer? Huh-uh, Clint. It was a good try, but it won't work. Who is back there? Mary?"

Clint looked quickly past the sheriff, hoping his eyes wouldn't give him away. He tensed for the lunge at the drawer . . .

Suddenly, loudly, from behind Jaime came the sound of a gun being cocked. The sound was unmistakable. Clint took a step toward the sheriff. "Drop it, Jaime. That scattergun could cut you in two."

The sheriff hesitated. He seemed about to whirl. Then, suddenly, he let the gun slide out of his grasp. It clattered on the floor. Clint walked to it, kicked it and sent it sliding halfway across the room.

"You can turn now, Jaime."

The sheriff turned his head. He smiled ruefully. "I thought it was you, Mary, but I wasn't sure. I couldn't take the chance."

Clint stared at the sheriff's face. "You're a liar," he said softly. "You knew it was her all the time. You just figured you'd rather lose than take a shot at her."

Jaime shrugged fatalistically.

Clint glanced beyond him at Mary, standing just inside the door. He walked to her and gently took the shotgun out of her hand. "Thank you, Mrs. Lamb," he said, as formally as though she had been a stranger who had just handed him a cup of tea. Yet there was a strong, underlying feeling in his voice that she could hear if the sheriff could not.

She was trembling violently. Her eyes were frightened. She asked with breathless terror, "Is Morgan all right?"

"He's all right. He's with Ellen Candelario."

"Then I'll go back. Thank you, Clint."

She turned and disappeared through the open door. Clint swung around toward Jaime Candelario. "You'll have to go back without your gun. I'm sorry, Jaime."

Jaime shrugged again. His face was sober as he said, "You'd better give yourself up, Clint. You and Kehoe and Morgan too. Too many people have been looking for an excuse too long. And I won't have a range war in my county like they

91

had in Lincoln County. I'll call in troops from Santa Fe first."

Clint didn't answer him. Candelario studied his face for a long, long time. At last he said, almost reluctantly, "Three days. You got three days. If you haven't surrendered yourself by then . . . I'm going to wire Santa Fe." He turned and walked to the door. With his hand on the knob, he said, "When I come in without you . . . I won't swear I can keep the lid on for three hours, let alone three whole days."

He went out. A moment later Clint heard his horse clatter out of the courtyard.

Deliberately he crossed the room and picked up Jaime's gun. He dropped it into a drawer of the desk, scowling. Damn Kehoe! Those three men of Parfet's . . . their deaths might have conceivably been smoothed over. But Parfet's death . . . Parfet shot from behind . . . That was a different breed of cat.

There was only one way to play this out. He'd have to fight. Unless he could find Kehoe and make him admit that the responsibility had been all his.

He crossed to the door and stepped out onto the gallery. Again he had the feeling Mary was standing there in her door. But this time he walked that way. He wouldn't touch her. He hadn't for nearly twenty years. Nor would he be less than formally polite. But between them would

92

pass a current of understanding, of support . . .

She came out and leaned against one of the great pine poles that supported the gallery roof. For a moment neither spoke. Then she said, "Tell me what's happening, Clint. All I hear is rumors and I don't know how much of what I hear is true."

"When Morgan left," Clint began, "I wanted to be sure he didn't have trouble getting across Parfet's land. I sent Kehoe with some men to see that he made it through. I guess Kehoe wanted to see him beaten up. So he waited, and by the time he interfered, Parfet's men figured they had gone too far. They put up a fight and three of them were killed. Kehoe left and I suppose Morgan helped Luke load the men. Anyway, Parfet was shot in the back someplace between where the fight took place and home. The sheriff has a warrant charging Morgan with that. He has warrants for Kehoe and for me charging the deaths of the other three."

"What are you going to do?"

"I'm not going to surrender myself. I can't. If I do, there won't be any Sombrero when I get out."

She was silent for a moment, and at last she asked softly, "Do you know where Morgan is? Clint, what will they do to him?"

"He's all right. I don't know where he is, but he's with Ellen Candelario."

"Could Kehoe find him? I'm afraid . . ."

Clint had thought of the same thing. If Kehoe would shoot Parfet in the back in the hope Morgan would be blamed, he was capable of killing Morgan too. But he said, "I wouldn't worry about it. Kehoe's got enough trouble on his hands without hunting Morgan down. Besides, I'm not even sure he could. This is a big country and Ellen knows it like a book."

Again there was silence, broken by her soft, "He's a fine boy, isn't he, Clint? He's so like you . . ." She stopped suddenly, and Clint said awkwardly, "Yes, he is a fine boy. I wish he could have stayed. Maybe . . ."

Almost angrily he said, "We never say what we mean, do we, Mary? We say everything else, but we never say what we mean." It was the first time he had called her Mary in almost twenty years.

"I should never have stayed. I should have gone away. We made one mistake together, but I have made many others since, mistakes I would not have made if I'd had the courage to go away."

"I thought . . ."

"Yes. I suppose it is what I wanted you to think. That my marriage vows were sacred to me, that I stayed out of respect for them. I had myself convinced it was true. But it was only partly true. Mostly I stayed because I could not face living away from where you were."

"Mary . . . I . . ."

"No! Don't touch me, Clint. Please don't touch me."

He stopped. He realized that his hands were trembling. He said harshly, "How do people make such messes of their lives? It's almost as though that was what they wanted to do. It's almost as though they tried."

Her voice was scarcely audible. "They do things they are ashamed of. And they try to make up for it. But making up for things must be the wrong way, Clint. Maybe it would be better if they could just forget the mistakes they've made and go on from there."

"Kehoe would never have let you forget."

"I'm not so sure of that, Clint. If I'd gone away . . . perhaps he would have followed me. Perhaps away from Sombrero . . . from you . . ."

He shrugged. He found himself thinking of Jane Redd, and cursed angrily to himself. When he wanted Mary most, he always went to Jane instead. And came away from Jane feeling frustrated and angry with himself because he knew he had hurt her. She loved him, he realized, and she deserved something better than an adobe house out on the empty reaches of Sombrero range. Just as Mary deserved something better than what she'd had all these years.

But it was too late—too late for Mary, too late for Jane.

He had a sudden, almost overpowering feeling

of dread. As though some part of his mind had caught a sudden glimpse of disaster, as though he'd had a premonition that someone he loved was going to die.

Not Mary, he thought. Not Mary or Morgan. Oh God . . . But he knew. He was afraid for both their lives and with Kehoe running loose there was plenty of reason for his fear.

# 10

Standing this close to him, Mary could feel the strength, the power emanating from him. As always, his attraction was almost overpowering. And yet, today, she felt something else. She felt his need.

She murmured hastily, "I've got to . . . I can't . . ." She couldn't finish and almost ran for her door. If she stayed out here a moment longer . . .

She went inside and closed the door behind her. She leaned against it weakly, trembling.

She tried to think of other things, without success. He would go to Jane now, she thought. Yet if she felt anger it was not toward Jane but toward herself.

She had told Clint the truth a few moments before. Today for the first time in twenty years, she had admitted to him and to herself that she had not stayed here with Kehoe because of respect for her marriage vows but because she could not bear to think of leaving Clint, never to see him again, never to hear his voice . . .

And now, she admitted something else. She and not Kehoe had been the destructive force all these many years. By remaining, feeling as she did, she had stolen from Kehoe any chance he might have had to forget. She had kept him hating, and remembering, until hate and memory warped and twisted his mind.

Nor had she helped Clint. If she'd gone away, he'd have found someone else and would have lived his life normally the way a man as male as Clint was meant to live. Perhaps it would not have been Jane Redd. But it would have been someone who loved him. And someone whom he loved.

She had destroyed Kehoe, and Clint, and herself. Perhaps she had destroyed Morgan too. If anything happened to Morgan because of this . . .

She must leave, she thought. Whether she wanted to or not, she must leave very soon. Self-deception had made it possible for her to remain before, but now the self-deception was gone.

She stumbled across the room and sat down weakly in a chair. She stared emptily at the door. "You must leave him," her mind said, "you must." And she thought of what it would be like to grow old never seeing him, never hearing his voice, never feeling his thoughts and his love, never being close enough to know his trouble and torment.

She got up and began to pace back and forth across the floor. There would be trouble and torment in him for a while if she left, she thought. But he would heal. He would find someone who could give him more than dreams and memories and not torment him the way she had.

And what about Morgan? What about their son? Would he stay here with Clint, or would he go with her? She'd want him, but she'd want him to stay here too. Where he would grow into the kind of man Clint was.

She began to tremble, terrified by the bleak gray loneliness she faced. Yet in spite of her terror, her resolve remained unwavering. She would only wait until she knew both Clint and Morgan were safe. Then she would go. She began to weep, softly, her shoulders shaking with her sobs.

In Clint, as the door closed behind her, there was a sudden overpowering feeling of loss. As though she had already gone from Sombrero, as though she were already gone out of his life.

He shook his head angrily and went back into the house. He sat down and stared moodily at the window. He closed his eyes, remembering that night so long ago.

He must have dozed off even though he hadn't intended to. When he wakened the room was dark. The clock said it was well past ten o'clock.

Clint hesitated a moment, thinking of Mary and of Jane. Then he slammed out the door and strode purposefully across the courtyard, through the gate and beyond. He went straight to Pete Candelario's house and hammered on the door. Pete answered it, wearing a cotton nightshirt.

"Get the men together first thing in the morning," Clint said. "Tell them I want Kehoe. Tell them to bring him in any way they can, but to bring him in."

"What if he puts up a fight?" Pete rubbed his eyes sleepily. "Come on inside."

Clint went in. Tonight he needed talk.

Pete left the door open to the cool night air. He rummaged around and finally found a brown bottle. He poured Clint a drink and one for himself.

"I don't want anyone killed, if that's what you mean," Clint said. "If one of the men spots him and can't take him alone, let him come back here for help."

"You think Kehoe's after Morgan?"

Clint shrugged almost angrily. "I don't know what to think. But he might have that on his mind."

There was a brief silence. Then Pete said, "Jaime stopped here on his way back to town.

He's worried. He thinks he may end up with a range war on his hands, like the one they had in Lincoln County. He says the only way to avoid it is for you and Kehoe and Morgan to come in. He says if you don't he'll bring troops out here and take you in."

"And what kind of a trial does he think we'll get?" Clint asked bitterly. "Where the hell would they get a jury, except out of the bunch that would like to slice Sombrero up?"

"Morgan might get off."

Clint nodded. "Yeah." He got up. "Keep six or eight men around all day tomorrow in case our neighbors get any big ideas."

"Sure, Clint. Good night."

Clint grunted and went outside. He hesitated briefly, then, as though he had made up his mind suddenly, strode to the corral and caught himself a horse. He saddled the animal with one of the saddles hanging from the fence, mounted and headed north.

It had been inevitable, of course, that a hatred as consuming as Kehoe's would ultimately bring them all to the brink of disaster. If it hadn't happened this way, it would have happened some other way. Yet this feeling that events were out of his control was new to Clint, and disturbing. He wrestled savagely with the problem in his mind, but came up with no solutions. There was really nothing he could do—about Kehoe's unpredictable madness—about Sombrero's enemies, bent on revenge for the four deaths. He could fight, and would, because that was what he had always done. But he couldn't fight off the feeling that he was doomed to lose.

The miles of darkness flowed beneath his horse's hoofs. This route was very familiar to him; he had traveled it many times. It was past midnight when he reached Jane's adobe house.

It was dark. He rode in, tied his horse and approached the door. He started when he saw Jane sitting in a rocker on the gallery.

She was clad in a white nightgown. "I couldn't sleep," Jane said softly.

She rose as he stepped beneath the gallery roof and preceded him through the door. She lighted a lamp, lowered the chimney and trimmed the wick. She turned to look at him.

She was younger than Clint by about ten years, and shorter by half a foot. Her hair, brown and shining, hung almost to her waist. She murmured soberly, "I hoped you would come, Clint."

He walked to her and put his big hands on her shoulders. He stared down into her face. Suddenly his arms went out and crushed her to him, hungrily, almost savagely. Her body, clad only in the thin nightgown, was warm and soft, and trembling.

He held her for a long, long time. It wasn't fair to come to Jane like this, he was thinking. To come to Jane, wanting only Mary. To make her a substitute because Mary was beyond his reach.

He drew away and stared down into her face. There were tears in her eyes.

"I'm sorry," he said. "I'm sorry for what I've done to you."

She laid her cheek against his chest. "Don't torment yourself so, Clint. I know. I've always known. The years teach us one thing, if nothing else—that no one gets everything they want. I have a part of you, Clint. I have a part that no one else can ever have."

His arms tightened again. Jane's trembling ceased. The tears remained in her eyes, but a small soft smile touched her lips.

She disengaged herself gently from his arms. She crossed the room and blew out the lamp. Then, in the still, warm darkness she returned to Clint.

# 11

Ellen rode in the lead when they left her uncle's house. But she did not ride fast. Instead, she held her horse to a steady trot, a gait he could maintain for hours without getting tired.

It was a hard gait for Morgan, though. A bone-jolting gait, one that had every bruise, every abrasion hurting him before they had gone a mile.

She headed east, behind the house, at first. She rode in this direction for several miles until she reached a long, wooded ridge where scrub pine and cedars grew abundantly. Here she took to the ridge, winding along its side, staying on the thick carpet of needles beneath the trees.

To Morgan, it was a weird world of twisted shapes that continued endlessly. The ridge gave way to another ridge, and another, and by the time Morgan realized they had changed directions, they were headed west.

They crossed the road leading to Sombrero in late afternoon, cautiously, at a place where it bridged a wide, dry wash. Ellen looked both ways along the road before she emerged from the trees, then let her horse pick his careful way along the rocky bottom of the wash.

She did not often speak to Morgan, but she did glance at him occasionally and glance quickly away. Once she let her horse slow to a walk, and another time she stopped, and dismounted, and motioned for Morgan to do the same.

There was tension between them. And strain. But it was born of the attraction they both felt and, Morgan knew, would eventually go away.

He wondered where the sheriff was. Had he gone out to Sombrero yet? Had he tried arresting Clint and Kehoe Lamb? He wondered, too, what would be accomplished in the end by his own flight. He couldn't elude the sheriff forever.

Nor could he stay out here alone with Ellen indefinitely.

He grinned faintly to himself, wondering what her parents would think of this. They certainly wouldn't approve. He had heard that Spanish girls were raised even more strictly than the girls back home.

Eventually Jaime Candelario would catch up with them, no matter how successfully Ellen hid their trail. Or they would have to return. Then facing the charge against him would be forced on him. And he, with Clint and Kehoe Lamb, would go on trial.

What all this local conflict was about, Morgan didn't know. He knew Clint was hated, by virtually everyone. How he had earned that hatred, he didn't know for sure, but he had heard enough to know that Clint was supposed to be pretty heavy-handed. Particularly about holding onto what belonged to him.

The land began to change as they continued west, as they left Sombrero range. It became more rocky. The grass was shorter and there was less timber. The vegetation gave way to sagebrush and later to clumps of a greenish, spiny brush Ellen said was greasewood.

And here the land was eroded more. Here it was cut with dry washes, which Ellen rode in whenever she could because the bottoms were almost always rocky and would hide their tracks.

Once, Morgan saw a small adobe shack in the distance. Once he saw a small bunch of cattle, shaded up against the afternoon sun in a thick clump of brush.

Shortly before sundown, they began to climb, toward a range of mountains whose tops still held patches of winter snow. And a little later they came to a tumbling, mountain stream.

Ellen put her horse into it immediately, climbed out on the far side, then deliberately backed her horse into it again. She turned upstream, keeping the horse in the water, and motioned for Morgan to follow her.

He did. It was cooler at this higher altitude and the water from the stream, when the horse splashed it up on him, was like ice. Dusk crept into the canyon, settling almost like a fog. It was nearly dark when Ellen finally rode her horse out of the water, picked her way through the timber for a ways, and stopped.

By the rapidly fading light, Morgan could see that they were in a small clearing. And that there was a cabin here . . .

It was built of logs and had an almost flat roof covered with dirt out of which high weeds grew. There was a tie-rail in front of it. Ellen dismounted and tied her horse. Morgan followed suit.

"We'll need some wood," she said.

"All right. I'll get it." He walked to the fringe

of timber that surrounded the clearing and began to gather wood. He gathered three or four good loads. By the time he had finished the last, Ellen had a fire going and was starting to prepare a meal.

The only light in the cabin was that which came from the open fireplace. He watched it flicker on her face, grown pink both from the heat and from the knowledge that he was watching her.

"Why do they hate him?" he asked.

"Your fa—?" She stopped, then said, "Clint? Why does a hungry man hate another who is full?"

"Is that the only reason?"

"No, I guess not. Parfet hated him because of Jane. Jane Redd. Parfet was seeing her and Clint took her away from him."

"There must be more to it than things like that."

She turned her head. "I suppose there is. Clint hanged two of his neighbors for stealing Sombrero horses once. He shot up some others who drove off a bunch of cattle. But mostly I think they hate him because he has so much. And because they want part of it."

"Was Jane Redd the reason Parfet tried to close the road?"

"Yes, I suppose she was."

"What's she like?"

She studied his face briefly. Then she said, "Not

what you'd expect. I like her. I feel sorry for her. And don't you get to blaming your father because he's seeing her. He's a man. And he's been eating his heart out over your mother for almost twenty years." Her voice was so militant that he couldn't help but smile.

The smile seemed to anger her even more. "What are you grinning at?"

His smile widened. "What are you getting so mad about? I didn't say a word."

"Yes, but you were thinking . . ." She stopped suddenly. Her anger disappeared. Confusion touched her eyes. "Come on and eat," she said.

He went to the fireplace and took the plate she handed him. It contained spiced pinto beans. He sat down in front of the fireplace and she gave him a tin cup filled with black coffee. She filled a plate for herself and sat down facing him.

He ate ravenously and, when she refilled his plate, finished that too. He set the plate aside and sipped the coffee. "How long can we stay out here? How long can we keep your uncle from finding us?"

"As long as we want to, if we keep moving all the time." There was strain in her voice and her eyes evaded his. She put down her plate. "We'd better get some sleep. We have to get started at dawn."

"Are we going to sleep in here?"

"No. It's safer outside."

She pushed a few coals farther back into the fireplace with her boot. Then she went to the door.

Morgan followed. He wanted to touch her, to hold her, but he held himself rigidly under control. He wasn't going to repay her for all she'd done for him by . . . Yet the need remained and he could not help thinking about what it would be like . . .

She reached the door and stepped into the darkness outside. He followed, stumbled, and crashed against her.

She staggered and nearly fell. He recovered his balance, reached out and caught her automatically.

How it happened . . . what happened . . . he hardly understood. Yet suddenly she was in his arms and her mouth was against his own . . . He knew he should not . . . yet suddenly he lifted her and carried her toward the concealment of the trees . . .

That movement . . . it was all that saved them both. Flame licked out from a rifle muzzle fifty feet away like the darting tongue of a poisonous snake. The report roared, reverberating afterward from the surrounding hills.

Morgan broke into a run, reached the trees and put Ellen down. His mind struggled to comprehend what was happening.

"Someone . . ." Ellen whispered, "someone

must have seen us and followed us. I know they couldn't have followed our trail."

"But who . . . ?" He immediately knew the answer to that. Only one person in the whole of Santiago County hated him enough to kill. Kehoe Lamb.

Ellen was trembling violently—he thought from fear—but when her voice came it was not afraid. It was furious. "The guns . . . the rifle you brought . . . the one I brought . . . they're both back there on the saddles."

For an instant he was silent. They had to have guns. Without them it was only a matter of time—until Kehoe caught up with them—and they would have no defense.

"I'll make enough noise to get him to following me," he whispered. "You circle around and get the guns. I'll work my way back to you. Come to this spot and hide. Wait for me."

She started to protest, but he put a hand over her mouth. Her voice was so soft it almost seemed he had imagined it, "Be careful, Morgan."

He began to run, making no effort to conceal the sounds he made. He crashed into a dead spruce branch and it cracked like a pistol shot. Grinning tightly and nervously, he rounded it and went on.

He had gone nearly a hundred yards before he stopped. The creek was near him now and it made a steady roar. The air was almost cold.

A sound back there . . . A soft sound but one he could roughly place as well this side of the spot he had left Ellen . . . He felt himself growing angry at the cold-bloodedness of the lurking killer. He knew certainly that if this was Kehoe Lamb then Kehoe was also the killer of Parfet.

He went on again, toward the creek, letting his passage through the remaining trees be a noisy one. He reached the stream bank and immediately stopped running and walked carefully along its bank.

He continued this way for over two hundred yards, then stopped and listened for a second time.

He was managing to stay ahead of Kehoe, at least, due perhaps to Kehoe's certainty that he had all the time he needed. Perhaps, he thought with sudden dismay, there was a reason for Kehoe's certainty. Perhaps Kehoe had their guns. He might have taken them from the saddles while he and Ellen were inside the cabin eating.

He'd know soon, he thought. He turned away from the stream bank, thinking that its roar in Kehoe's ears would, for now at least, conceal the sounds he might be unable to avoid going through the trees toward the cabin again.

He moved carefully, straining his eyes in the darkness so that he could avoid the obstacles. Once, a small branch cracked beneath his feet. Spruce limbs, brushing against him, made an unavoidable rustling. Then, suddenly, he was in the clearing and could see the glow of the fire through the open cabin door.

He headed across the clearing at a trot toward the place he had left Ellen. But before he reached it, he saw her at one corner of the cabin . . .

He ran toward her, hearing as he did the plain cocking of a rifle there.

Had he made a mistake? Had Kehoe beaten him here? He called, softly and almost frantically, "Ellen?"

He saw the rifle lowered, and an instant later was beside her. She thrust a rifle into his hands. "It's cocked and loaded. I . . . I thought you were him."

"Could you see . . . when he went past you . . . ?"

"Not very well. But I think it's Kehoe Lamb."

"Stay here in the shadows. I'm going back."

"No . . . Please . . ."

But he had already gone. He stepped out away from the cabin wall, started across the clearing . . .

The rifle spat from the timber's edge. He heard the bullet tear a furrow in the ground at his feet. He flung himself flat on the ground.

He heard a scream. A second rifle roared from beside the cabin . . . He jerked his head around . . .

Ellen was running toward him, silhouetted against the light filtering softly from the

111

cabin door and spilling onto the ground in front. She made a perfect target for the hidden rifleman . . .

"Damn it, go back!" he yelled, rolling as he did, straining his eyes into the darkness, trying to see something that was invisible. His rifle was ready, and up, waiting for the flash over there, waiting for it and dreading it too.

Draw the man's fire, he thought. And tightened his finger on the trigger instantly.

His rifle roared, echoing from the tall hills nearby, and before the echoes had died away, he was rolling . . . away from that spot . . . but keeping his eyes on the fringe of timber at the clearing's edge.

The hidden rifle flared again, the bullet striking so close it showered Morgan with dirt. But he had a target now, and was ready for it to appear. He fired instantly at the flash.

He was rewarded by a shout—wordless—a startled cry of shock and pain. He got up and ran toward the spot.

He could hear a crashing in the brush and timber, retreating, fading. He stopped uncertainly at the timber's edge, wondering if he should go on.

Standing there, he heard an increased crashing, and a few moments later, the drumming of a horse's hoofs.

Whoever it had been was hit, though how

badly he had no idea. He turned and walked back toward the cabin.

Ellen met him halfway, running, breathless, scared . . . "Are you all right? Are you hurt?"

"I'm all right," he said as he put out his arms and held her a moment close against his chest. He could feel her trembling. He could remember the way she had run recklessly out from the cabin wall when she'd thought that he was hit . . .

He could remember too the way she had hidden herself while the stalker went past following him . . . And she'd successfully recovered the guns . . .

Different from the girls he'd known . . . she'd fight like a tigress for the man she loved . . .

"We don't dare stay here now," she said. "He might come back."

She struggled and he released her. She walked back toward the cabin.

Following her, he was almost glad he had been accused of killing Luke Parfet. If he had not been, he would have been hundreds of miles away by now, instead of here, with Ellen Candelario.

Neither spoke as they mounted their horses and picked a careful way through the timber to the stream. There was a new closeness between them now that did not need words.

# 12

Pounding away through the timber, Kehoe Lamb cursed savagely and vindictively. His left arm was numb from shoulder to elbow and he could feel blood running down his forearm and dripping from his finger tips.

He had no way of knowing immediately how bad it was. But he was losing blood, a lot of it. He had to get someplace . . . where he could build a fire and take care of it.

Damn! If Morgan hadn't picked that girl up and moved just as he fired . . . He wondered how the damn kid had known he was there . . .

But he'd have another chance. And next time he wouldn't miss.

He rode steadily downcountry for the better part of an hour. At last he reached a fairly level spot and stopped.

He slid from his horse and awkwardly tied the animal to a tree. He began to gather wood . . .

When he had enough, he started a fire in a bunch of twigs, adding larger pieces as the fire grew. When it was blazing well, he shed his jacket and stripped his sleeve up to uncover the wound, wincing with pain as he did.

Sight of the clean, small hole was vastly reassuring. The bullet hadn't even nicked the bone. It was a flesh wound and nothing more. It would be painful as hell for a couple of weeks and the arm wouldn't be much good for at least that long. But it wasn't going to incapacitate him. It wasn't going to stop him from seeking the vengeance he deserved.

He went to his horse, fumbled in the saddlebags a moment and returned to the fire carrying a brown bottle that was still half full. He sat down facing the fire and put the bottle on the ground in front of him. He unbuttoned his shirt and ripped a strip from the front of his underwear.

He removed the cork from the bottle and took a long drink. Afterward, he soaked the piece of underwear with whisky and wiped the wound with it. He tied the rag around the wound, awkwardly knotting it with one hand and his teeth. When he had finished, his face was pale. He took another long drink from the bottle, then corked it and put it aside.

For a long time, he stared moodily into the flames. His face was gaunt, but his eyes seemed to burn with a fire all their own. There was a three-day growth of whiskers on his face.

The fire gradually died to a bed of coals. Shivering, Kehoe got up, went to his saddle and got his blanket roll. He picketed the horse at the end of his rope, then returned to the fire and wrapped himself in his blankets near to it.

He lay for a while, staring at the stars. Parfet

and the others had apparently been found. And, as he had expected would be the case, Morgan had obviously been accused of killing Luke.

How he had escaped from Jaime Candelario, Kehoe couldn't guess. But apparently he had. And somehow he'd gotten together with Ellen . . .

With her helping him, Morgan would be hard to find a second time. He'd glimpsed them just by accident yesterday, and had followed them by sight. He would never have been able to catch them just by trailing them. Ellen concealed their trail too cleverly.

Nor was there much use returning to the isolated cabin and picking up their trail. It would be too slow. No. He'd have to outguess them if he was going to find them a second time.

But where would they go? Would Ellen lead Morgan aimlessly around the country? He doubted it. They'd either hole up someplace or they'd go to Sombrero.

Tomorrow, then, he'd ride a course between the cabin where he'd come upon them last night and the headquarters of Sombrero ranch. If he didn't cut their trail, he'd have to think of something else. But it was worth a try.

He fell into a feverish sleep, one that was filled with dreams and pain. He was charging up the hill at Gettysburg. He was fighting his way through a Carolina swamp. He was making his way back to New Mexico.

116

Then he dreamed he was fighting Clint Morgan, rolling, gouging, kicking, biting. And Clint had him by the throat . . .

He awoke, sweating, gasping as though he were out of breath. There was a faint line of gray silhouetting the horizon in the east.

He got up painfully, shivering from a sudden chill. He wondered briefly if dreams were prophetic, if Clint would really kill him in the end.

He shook his head almost angrily. No! Clint wasn't going to cheat him that way. Clint himself was going to die. But only after he had seen the dead body of his son, only after he had seen Kehoe kill Mary right before his eyes.

He mounted his horse and, still shivering violently both from the shock of his wound and the chill, rode away toward the north and east.

# 13

Jaime Candelario pushed hard through the night toward San Juan. He rarely resented the distances here, the time it took to go from place to place. It was a thing to be accepted because it could not be changed.

Yet in this situation he found himself growing impatient. Much could have happened in San Juan in the time he had been gone. Much could happen at Sombrero before he could get back to it.

Keeping the peace was normally a fairly simple and methodical thing. Someone broke the law and when they did, they fled. Jaime would get a saddle horse and a pack together and go after them. If they were dangerous or if there were more than a couple of them, he would get up a posse.

Sometimes it took a week, sometimes a month or more. He was good at trailing; he'd learned from Comanches. He knew the country as well as almost anyone. If he lost the trail, he could pretty well guess where the fugitives would go. And he nearly always caught them in the end.

But this was more complex than pursuing fugitives. This involved people who normally did not break the law. And Jaime was cursed with the ability to see right on both sides.

If he could catch Kehoe . . . that would probably calm things down for a while. But catching Kehoe might take weeks, because Kehoe knew the country even better than Jaime did.

And a man got tired. Good God, the ride out to Sombrero and back was close to two hundred miles. He hadn't been able to get any sleep since he'd left town, and he wouldn't dare take time for any until he got back. Maybe not even then.

It was late when he reached his brother Juan's adobe house. The buckboard was in the yard, so he knew they had returned from Parfet's place.

He dismounted stiffly and tied his horse. He hammered on the door and Juan answered it, carrying a lighted lamp. Juan said worriedly, "Ellen's gone. She was here when we left and she said she was going to stay but . . ."

"She's with Morgan Lamb," Jaime said. "I've got a warrant charging him with Parfet's death and he's on the run."

"Did he do it? He didn't seem . . ."

"Hell no, he didn't do it," Jaime said wearily. "If I was to guess I'd say Kehoe did. But it ain't up to me to decide who did what. I just do my job. How about something to eat? And a fresh horse."

"Sure. Go on in. I'll catch you a horse." Juan hesitated a moment, then handed Jaime the lamp. He untied the sheriff's horse and led him away toward the corral. Jaime went inside.

He sank wearily into a chair. His eyes closed. He dozed briefly while his brother's wrapper-clad wife put food in front of him. She shook his shoulder gently and he awoke. He ate almost numbly. Finished, he thanked her in Spanish and went outside.

Juan was squatting in the gallery's darkness. The stars were bright and the air was fresh and cool. Jaime untied the fresh horse's reins, mounted, and turned away. He halted a dozen yards from the house, turned his head and said,

"Watch out for Kehoe if he comes here, Juan. He . . . well, he could be dangerous."

Juan nodded. Jaime rode away toward town, letting the horse lope until he was tired enough to stop. After that he held him to a steady, mile-eating trot.

At the spot the fracas had occurred, Morgan's dead horse lay, bloating now.

He stopped for a moment, staying to windward of the horse, and tried to see enough to decide what had really happened here. Shaking his head, he went on. Morgan might have been pushed far enough to kill, he thought, but if Morgan was anything like Clint, he wouldn't have followed Parfet and shot him in the back. That was a coldly premeditated act of murder and it didn't fit with Jaime's estimate of Morgan at all.

It all looked like Kehoe's work to him. Kehoe was the one corroded and soured with hate. Kehoe was capable of starting a senseless blood bath, like the killing of Parfet's three men. He was also capable of cold-blooded murder. He was capable of killing Morgan, and Clint, and even his own wife.

Maybe he could calm that hotheaded bunch down when he got back to town. If he could, it might pay to get up a posse and go after Kehoe Lamb.

It was dawn when he reached San Juan. He had

120

been dozing, and the early noises of the town woke him up.

He could see that they had been waiting for him to return. Nearly every saloon in town was still going strong. He could also see that they were furious because he was returning without prisoners.

They came shuffling out of the doors of the saloons. They followed him down the street, in small groups that welded themselves into a single group as they drew closer to the jail. Jaime could hear Nate Duffy yelling at them, but he couldn't make out all of what Duffy said.

He heard enough, however, to make him scowl sourly at the approaching group as he dismounted stiffly in front of the jail. He tied his horse and turned to face them, irritable, tired, angry because he had to spend time reasoning with a bunch of unreasonable men instead of just going in and trying to get some badly needed sleep.

"Where the hell are your prisoners?" Nate bawled. "Don't tell us they got away!"

Jaime didn't reply. He waited until they were close enough to hear words spoken in a normal tone of voice. Then he said, "Nobody takes Clint Morgan unless he wants to be taken. Not in the house at Sombrero anyway." It sounded lame and it was lame. And he admitted something to himself he had not been willing to admit before. He *could* have taken Clint if he'd really tried.

He *could* have kept Morgan in custody earlier.

Duffy glared at him furiously. "It's pretty damn plain where you stand, Candelario. It looks like we're going to have to take care of this job all by ourselves."

"Shut up, Nate. You're talking like a kid," Jaime said wearily.

"Kid, am I? You spick son-of-a-bitch . . ."

Jaime was a patient man. He had been born on the edge of Sombrero, where Juan lived now. His parents and grandparents had lived and died within two hundred miles of here while Duffy's were cutting peat and fighting among themselves five thousand miles away in Old Erin.

Or maybe it wasn't the word "spick" that really enraged him at all. Maybe it was the contempt with which it was spoken. As though Jaime Candelario were the interloper here. As though Duffy belonged.

He moved like a striking rattlesnake. He was five paces from Duffy when the man spoke. Before the words were out, he had reached Duffy and had his gun in his hand.

Fist and fisted gun jabbed cruelly at Duffy's midsection. As the man doubled, as he expelled a surprised grunt of pain, Jaime's gun barrel rapped him solidly on the back of the head.

Jaime stepped back, ready for any further trouble that might develop. He said thinly, "Drag the Irish bastard into a cell. *You,* and *you!*"

Those he had indicated moved forward sullenly to pick up Duffy's arms as Jaime said, "Carleson, pick up his hat and bring it in."

He turned contemptuously and followed the skidding body of Duffy into the jail. He took Duffy's hat when Carleson brought it in, walked back to the cell they had dragged Duffy into, and tossed the hat in on the floor. He followed the pair out to the office, but stopped them before they shuffled out the door. "Tell that rabble out there to go home. Unless they want to end up where Duffy is."

He slammed the door behind them, and shot the bar into place. He stood there groggily for an instant, swaying with weariness.

He hadn't handled them very well, he knew. Duffy had taken the lead in swearing out the warrants and he had been their spokesman a few minutes before. But Duffy wasn't the only angry one. There were others among them that could easily take Duffy's place.

He stumbled back to Duffy's cell, slammed and locked the steel, barred door. He returned to the office and tossed the key on the desk. He crossed to the office couch. If he could sleep a couple of hours . . . If he could only close his eyes for just a little while . . .

The cot creaked as he literally fell on it. And he was instantly asleep.

• • •

The sun was up when he awoke. He was sweating heavily. He lay there groggily for several moments, wondering what had awakened him.

Outside the jail he could hear a faint buzz . . . the combined sounds of many voices. He seemed to remember closer sounds, as though he had dreamed them . . . whispering voices . . . other, rasping sounds.

He leaped to his feet. He hurried back to Duffy's cell . . .

Duffy was gone. So were two of the bars to his cell window. Jaime hadn't dreamed those whispering voices. Nor had he dreamed the rasping sounds of a hacksaw cutting through the bars.

He returned to the office and went to the door. He opened it and stepped outside. The last of them were just trooping into Lew Connors' saloon halfway down the street.

He closed the door, crossed the room and sat down at his desk. He shook his head almost angrily. He was too groggy from sudden awakening to think very clearly immediately. And he didn't want to face that bunch until his mind was clear, until he had decided what he was going to do.

He was suddenly glad Morgan had gotten away from him, glad too that he hadn't brought Clint in a prisoner. In the mood that bunch was in . . . if they'd saw Duffy out of jail . . . They might do anything. They might even try taking the law into their own hands. Particularly since every one of them was aware that only Clint Morgan, alive, stood between them and the rich, vast acres of Sombrero range.

Briefly, Jaime Candelario considered the advisability of going down to Lew Connors' saloon and taking Duffy into custody a second time. It was what he wanted to do; it was what his position as sheriff demanded that he do. Yet he also knew that Duffy had become a symbol, a living symbol as much as Parfet was a dead one.

He got up and began to pace irritably back and forth across the office. Calling in troops from Santa Fe would be an admission that he couldn't handle the situation himself. He didn't like admitting it, even to himself. And yet he knew it was true. Duffy and that bunch of Sombrero's neighbors would eventually work themselves up to the point of riding out and attacking Sombrero headquarters. And Clint Morgan would fight them off. It was the only thing he could do.

Furthermore, there was Kehoe . . . and there was Morgan Lamb . . .

Jaime picked up his hat. He checked his gun and seated it lightly in its holster. He went to the door and stepped outside.

The sun was hot already and the air was still.

Jaime tramped through town to the railroad station, where the telegraph office was. He went inside, reached for a blank and a pencil stub and quickly scrawled his message. REQUEST TROOPS TO RESTORE ORDER. URGENT. He signed his name and wrote beneath it: SHERIFF, SANTIAGO COUNTY, NEW MEXICO.

He put the pencil down and stared at the scrawled message. Perhaps he was a fool for sending it. Perhaps there would be no range war, no attack on Sombrero at all. Perhaps the bunch down there in Lew Connors' saloon would just get tanked up on whisky and go home to sleep it off.

Jaime frowned indecisively. He didn't really believe it. He didn't believe Duffy's bunch was as harmless as that.

Four men were already dead. He couldn't reason that fact away. Suddenly he said, "Send this right away," and shoved the message across the desk at the operator.

The man read it, glanced worriedly up at Jaime, then looked away. Jaime felt a strange compulsion to defend himself and it angered him. He turned away and stalked angrily out onto the station platform.

It was done. Mistake or no, it was done. Now he could go ahead and do what he felt he had to do.

He walked almost reluctantly back up the

street toward Lew Connors' saloon. Sending that message, he thought, had all but doomed any chance he might have had to continue as sheriff here. If he failed to take Duffy into custody again . . . He was through for good.

Walking, he licked his lips nervously. And scowled at his own nervousness.

He wasn't afraid, he told himself. He wasn't afraid of anything they could do to him. He'd faced a good many lawbreakers without feeling this uncertainty, this clamminess, this coldness in his spine.

It was failure he feared, he realized. What he was really afraid of was that they'd defy him and refuse to let him take Duffy away from them. But he knew too that even if he failed, he had to try.

He reached the doors of Connors' saloon. They were open and from them drifted the odor of tobacco smoke and the smell of whisky. They were a noisy bunch. It was hard to distinguish a single voice from the babble of talk mingling and drifting through the doors . . .

The sheriff stepped inside. He waited silently. The quiet spread from those closest him until at last it had touched every man in the saloon. "Duffy, you're under arrest," Jaime said evenly. "Clasp your hands behind your head and walk this way."

For several long moments, no one moved. No sound broke the silence.

Then a murmur of protesting voices began, a grumbling that Jaime knew would grow if he allowed it to. "Shut up!" he said sharply. "I want Duffy. If anybody butts into this, I'll take him too for jailbreaking and resisting arrest."

The murmur quieted, but only briefly, and when it began again Jaime knew that he had lost. Duffy stepped out of the crowd, stood alone for a moment, then was joined by half a dozen others. Duffy glanced around at them. When he turned back to Jaime, he was grinning. "Take seven of us, Candelario. Take all seven of us if you can."

Jaime's hand hung poised over the grips of his holstered gun. He could kill Duffy, he realized. Perhaps he could get a couple of the others too. But it wouldn't stop them from what they meant to do. It wouldn't keep them from riding out to Sombrero and attacking it. It would only pile more fuel upon the flames of their determination because they would blame these killings on Clint Morgan too.

"You're making a mistake—all of you," he said. "There'll be warrants out for you. When the troops arrive the warrants will be served."

"You've sent for troops?" Duffy's face showed his sudden concern.

Jaime nodded.

Duffy turned his head. "Then we'd better get going," he yelled, "if we're going to get it done before the troops arrive!"

They all began to move and talk at once. Jaime stepped aside and watched as they trooped out of the saloon. He felt the strong, sour taste of defeat.

He'd tried taking Duffy and he'd failed. And he'd given away information that had only succeeded in making things worse.

Not that they'd have remained in ignorance very long. Someone would have learned about the telegraph message he'd sent a few moments before.

Wearily he stepped outside after the last of them. He stood and watched them as they headed for the livery barn.

He felt older than he ever had before as he walked along the street toward the jail. It was out of his hands now. There was nothing more he could do until the troops arrived. And by then it would probably be too late.

# 14

As before, Ellen Candelario rode in the lead. Morgan followed a dozen feet behind.

Even in almost complete darkness, she seemed to know exactly where she was, seemed to know as well what was immediately ahead of her. From the sound of his horse's hoofs against the ground underfoot, sometimes rocky, sometimes soft and spongy with fallen pine needles, sometimes watery, Morgan knew they were leaving little trail and sometimes no trail at all. Kehoe couldn't follow them. At least he couldn't trail.

The hours passed slowly. Morgan drowsed wearily in his saddle. The days since his arrival had been hard. He'd been beaten twice. He'd slept only one whole night. His meals had been irregular and he'd missed several of them.

At midnight, atop a rocky point that over-looked the vast plain, Ellen stopped. "We'll camp here until morning and see if we can't get a little sleep," she said.

Morgan dismounted and tied his horse securely to a stout clump of brush. Ellen was taking her saddle off, so Morgan followed suit. Before he had finished, Ellen had wrapped herself in blankets and was lying on the ground, her head pillowed on her saddle.

Morgan lay down not far away. The saddle made a hard pillow, but he could have pillowed his head on a rock tonight. He stared into the darkness toward Ellen for several moments before he closed his eyes.

When he did, he was instantly asleep and he did not wake until Ellen shook his shoulder at dawn. "We'd better get down off this point before it gets very light."

He got up, rolled his blankets and tied them behind his saddle. He saddled his horse, untied the reins and mounted, following Ellen as she picked a precarious way down the rocky slope.

While Morgan was groggy with sleep and still not fully awake, he realized that he couldn't continue with Ellen this way. Not indefinitely. Last night she could have been killed. Or badly hurt. Yet he also knew he'd have a difficult time persuading her to let him go on alone.

When they reached the level plain, Ellen immediately angled off to one side so that she could travel in a long, low depression and thus remain unseen from the surrounding plain.

The sun came up, warming their chilled bodies. Morgan began to feel less depressed and more cheerful than he had before. And for the first time he felt anticipation—a certain excitement at the prospect of matching wits with those who would like to kill or capture him.

Sometimes Ellen would cross a ridge but she stayed in the low areas as much as she could. After an hour of steady traveling she stopped suddenly beside a small alkali stream. "I want some coffee. Let's stop for a few minutes and eat."

Morgan gathered wood, careful that it was dry so that its burning would make less smoke. He built a fire, watching it carefully. Ellen arranged the smoke-blackened coffeepot so that it would heat. Without looking up she said, "I think you ought to go back to Sombrero. Clint and your

131

mother are probably worried sick wondering if you're all right."

He was silent for a moment. He didn't want to go to Sombrero. He didn't want Clint to think he was running to him for protection from the law. But he knew that if he did return, at least Ellen would be safe.

He nodded finally. "I suppose I should. How far is it from here?"

"We could be there by midafternoon."

"Let's go then." He took the coffee and beans she had prepared and ate hungrily, watching her as he did.

Again he felt the strong pull of attraction and knew she was feeling it too. She glanced up at him once, then glanced quickly away.

While she washed the utensils they had used with sand in the narrow stream, Morgan scattered the fire. They remounted and continued toward Sombrero headquarters.

The sun climbed slowly across the sky. The air was clear and fresh, smelling faintly of the scrub sage their horses sometimes trampled underfoot. He realized suddenly that he did not want to leave this country, even if staying didn't make much sense.

It could not have been foreseen . . . couldn't have been avoided, even though Ellen blamed herself later for allowing it to happen. One instant they were riding alone, nearing Sombrero.

The next they were face to face with a group that must have contained nearly thirty men.

For an instant Ellen and Morgan stared at them dumfoundedly. The next they had wheeled and were racing away, while behind them raised eager shouts of, "There he is! There's one of 'em!"

A scattering of gunfire popped behind them like a string of firecrackers. Ellen turned her head and cried, "Lean forward! Get as low as you can!"

Morgan did, glancing behind immediately afterward. The group had spread out in a line so they could fire without endangering each other. Two or three were banging away uselessly with revolvers. But there were one or two with rifles . . .

Morgan veered away from Ellen, putting his horse twenty feet to the right of her. They wouldn't deliberately shoot at her, he realized. But they might hit her by mistake.

She turned her head and saw what he had done. Instantly she yanked her rifle from the saddle scabbard at her side. Turning in the saddle, she began to fire methodically.

Morgan glanced around again. He doubted if Ellen was trying to hit any of them. But they apparently thought she was. They began to drop back out of effective rifle range.

He veered over close to her again. She stopped firing and returned the rifle to its scabbard. Her black hair whipped out behind her in the wind.

She smiled at him briefly, but her eyes held a worried look.

"Is it a posse?" Morgan shouted. "Is the sheriff with them?"

"Do you think my uncle would have let them shoot at me?"

He turned his head. Dust raised from the hoofs of both his own and Ellen's horse. The pursuers were kicking up a lot of dust as well. But he saw one face . . . a face he had seen in town . . . one of those who had brought in Parfet and Parfet's men . . .

And he remembered the shout he'd heard: "There's one of 'em!"

These must be Sombrero's neighbors, then. Parfet's friends. Clint's enemies. If they were here on Sombrero range, armed, it meant they had been heading for Sombrero headquarters just as he and Ellen had.

At least, he thought, while they were pursuing Ellen and himself they couldn't attack Clint. But how long could he and Ellen stay ahead of them?

He turned his head, that question in his eyes. She shook her head and he saw that she had little hope. Before nightfall their horses would give out. And in darkness was their only chance.

The distance between them and their pursuers widened gradually. But not enough. Morgan's horse stumbled and almost fell.

Ellen reined her horse in, slowed him to a trot.

"They can't hold this pace any more than we can!" she shouted.

She veered sharply to the right, heading toward a long, dry wash. Reaching it, she plunged her horse over its precipitous side, raising a blinding cloud of dust.

Morgan followed, surprised that she had already dismounted by the time he reached her side. She yanked her rifle out and climbed the crumbly side of the wash.

Morgan followed suit. Ellen opened fire. A horse fell, and rolled, throwing his rider clear.

Morgan sighted carefully on one of the pursuer's horses. He squeezed off his shot and grinned to himself when the horse went down and lay kicking on his side.

The pursuers yanked their horses to a halt. For several moments they milled uncertainly. Ellen fired again.

This bullet kicked up a shower of dust immediately in front of them. They wheeled and retreated hastily.

Ellen was also smiling now. Her face was grimy and covered with dust. "Come on," she said. "By the time they realize we're not here any more we can be two or three miles away."

The pair mounted and Ellen led out along the wash, traveling slowly and carefully so that rising dust would not betray their progress. This way they traveled more than a mile. Then, where the wash flattened out, Ellen came out cautiously and, watching the group behind, rode over a knoll and into the lower land beyond.

Morgan glanced behind at the group as he went over the knoll. They were watching the place from which he and Ellen had fired at them. A smaller group was circling to come upon the spot from behind . . .

He began to feel a little hope. If they could reach rougher country . . . or if they could keep ahead until nightfall . . . they might yet get away.

But how many more such ruses could Ellen use? Next time the pursuing group would be on its guard.

More miles fell behind. Occasionally, unavoidably, they would glimpse the group, who were pursuing them again. Each time they did, Ellen immediately changed course and Morgan understood that she was trying to keep the pursuers trailing instead of following them by sight.

Shadows lengthened gradually. The sun dropped toward the ragged horizon in the west. At least, thought Morgan, the group couldn't attack Sombrero today. They'd wasted too much time chasing him.

He knew something else as well. Tonight—or tomorrow—he would go on alone. Somehow he'd get away from Ellen and go on by himself. He wasn't going to endanger her any more.

The sun dropped out of sight. The shadows of

dusk crept across the land. Ellen smiled at him reassuringly.

"Hadn't we better find someplace to get fresh horses as soon as it gets dark?" he said.

She nodded. "We'll go to my Uncle Juan's."

"Do you think they'll try to follow us tomorrow?"

She shook her head. "They'll give up. They'll go back."

"To Sombrero?"

She nodded. "That's where they were heading when they ran into us."

"Can Clint . . . ? How many men has he got?"

"Fifteen . . . twenty maybe. But don't worry about Clint. He knows how to take care of himself."

He wondered what the group of men would have done to him had they caught him earlier. Somehow or other he found it hard to believe that they'd simply have returned to town with him and turned him over to Jaime Candelario. No. It wouldn't have been as easy as that. Quite possibly they'd have hanged him from the first tree they were able to find. They'd have given him the same brand of justice Clint had given the horse thieves years before.

As soon as it was completely dark, Ellen turned her horse, setting a course, Morgan supposed, toward her Uncle Juan's.

And he knew suddenly how he was going to get

away from her. He'd offer to saddle fresh horses while she went to the house for food. He'd catch one fresh horse . . . for himself . . . and drive the others out of the corral.

She'd be furious, of course. But at least she would be safe.

They traveled steadily, though slowly because there wasn't much strength left in their horses. Stars brightened as the night progressed. Somewhere, on a nearby mesa, a pack of coyotes yipped and barked.

Morgan found himself wondering how all this was going to end. Kehoe Lamb was like a mad dog running loose. Kehoe alone had been responsible for the deaths of Parfet's three men because if he hadn't waited—if he hadn't started firing at them—they might have given up without a fight.

And Kehoe had murdered Parfet. There wasn't any doubt in Morgan's mind of that. Just as Kehoe had tried to murder him last night, not caring if he killed Ellen too.

Obviously, then, Kehoe had gone beyond the point where he could go back. The penalty for one murder was death by hanging. The penalty was no more severe for several murders.

He frowned to himself in the darkness. Kehoe was by no means the only problem. Sombrero's neighbors had also gone past the point where they could stop.

Morgan wondered where the sheriff was. Not that it mattered particularly. Jaime Candelario was helpless. No one man could control events in Santiago County now.

It was near to dawn when they finally reached Juan's place, coming upon it from the rear, from the hillside that sheltered it. The place was dark.

Before the door they dismounted. Morgan took the reins of Ellen's horse. "I'll catch fresh horses while you go in and get some food."

She hesitated and finally agreed silently by going into the house.

Swiftly now, Morgan led the two horses to the corral. He removed the sack containing food and cooking utensils from Ellen's saddle and transferred it to his own.

He unsaddled both horses and turned them loose. Then he went into the corral and caught the strongest-looking horse he could find.

He led the animal out, saddled him, then opened the corral gate. He mounted, rode in and eased the others out. When they were clear of the gate, and bunched, he let out a yell and spurred his horse into a gallop.

The horses thundered out of the yard and down the long draw in the direction of town. Morgan glanced once at the house and saw Ellen running toward him.

He didn't stop. He followed the galloping horses for a couple of miles to be sure they didn't stop. Then he reversed directions and rode north, staying well to the east of Juan Candelario's house.

He suddenly felt more alone than at any time in his entire life. He felt like a hunted animal. But he wasn't sorry for what he had done. This was his problem, not Ellen Candelario's. He would solve it in his own way, or be caught and killed. He wouldn't have her hurt doing something he ought to be able to do himself.

Dawn grayed the endless land briefly before the sun came up. Morgan stayed in the long, wide valleys and draws, as Ellen had done yesterday. But occasionally he would climb a knoll afoot and scan the country for as far as he could see.

He could not conceal his trail, as Ellen had. But he could guard himself against being surprised. And he could fight if he was caught.

# 15

When Jaime Candelario reached the jail, he went inside, not bothering to close the door. He stared glumly at the desk, piled high with papers, and at the gunrack beyond it.

This office was even more familiar to him than his home. All the years he had been sheriff were here, represented by different material things, guns, scarred furniture, papers, memories . . .

All in all, he told himself, his years as sheriff had been successful ones. He had kept the peace. He had made Santiago County both unsafe and uncomfortable for lawbreakers.

With the coming of Morgan Lamb, that had been changed. And now things were completely out of hand. Four men were dead and more would be dead before the troops arrived. Even if they left Santa Fe immediately—even if they traveled by forced march—they still would not arrive in time. The battle for Sombrero would be over and the victors would be in possession there.

He crossed the room wearily and sat down on the edge of the cot. He rubbed his whiskered face reflectively. Clint Morgan couldn't win. Clint couldn't get more than twenty men together to save his life. And there were over thirty in Duffy's group.

He laid back on the cot. The few hours sleep he'd had only made him feel the need for sleep more strongly. He closed his eyes . . .

He slept almost instantly. But he dreamed, and sweated, and tossed uneasily on the cot. He dreamed he was walking into the saloon again, intent on taking Duffy prisoner. Only this time he shot Duffy in the chest, and then two of the others before their bullets cut him down.

He awoke, soaked with sweat but chilled as well. The room was dark.

141

Something had awakened him. The door still stood ajar. A man stood framed in it . . .

Jaime's hand snatched for his gun. The hammer clicked as it came back.

He eased it down as he heard a voice, that of the telegraph operator's son Willy Bond. "Sheriff? It's me, Willy. I got an answer to your telegram."

"All right, Willy. Wait until I light a lamp." Jaime got up off the creaking cot, fumbling for a match. He raised the lamp chimney and touched the flame to the wick. He lowered the chimney and turned.

Bond handed him a yellow slip of paper. "They can't come. It says here they can't come."

"All right." Jaime took the paper and held it so that the lamp light shone on it. His eye skipped the heading and read the message itself. TROOPS CANNOT BE DISPATCHED WITHOUT THE AUTHORIZATION OF THE GOVERNOR, WHO CANNOT BE REACHED FOR SEVERAL DAYS. SUGGEST YOU TELEGRAPH HIM DIRECT. YOUR REQUEST WILL BE CONSIDERED UPON HIS RETURN.

Jaime wadded the paper into a ball and flung it angrily at the coal bucket beside the stove.

How would he have acted earlier today had he known the troops were not available, he wondered. Would he have stopped Duffy even if it meant killing him?

He nodded reluctantly, knowing that he would. And he faced a sour, unpalatable fact. He had let himself depend upon outside help. All the years he had been sheriff he had depended only upon himself. Until today. Briefly he wished he had today to live over again. But he didn't. What was done was done.

Willy Bond stared at him uneasily a moment, then turned and shuffled away. He disappeared into the darkness. Jaime crossed the room and closed the door.

For several minutes he paced back and forth across the office, scowling at the floor. The trouble was, he realized suddenly, that he had been considering this particular breach of the peace as something special merely because the participants didn't happen to be criminals. He should never have considered it as anything more or less than a simple breach of the peace. He should have dealt with it as such.

The law provided certain aids to a law-enforcement officer. It gave him the right to raise a posse and deputize its members. It made refusal to join a posse an offense . . .

Decisively, he crossed to the desk and blew out the lamp. He went to the door, opened it and stepped into the night outside. He was on familiar ground again and no longer undecided as to what he should do.

He headed for Lew Connors' saloon. He needed

a posse. He'd raise one from among the men of San Juan. They didn't dare refuse.

Yet when he stepped through the doors, he faced the crowd inside with less than his usual confidence. He crossed the room to the bar and turned.

The room quieted almost uneasily. Few of the men would meet his glance. He said clearly, "I want a dozen men for a posse. I want them ready to go in twenty minutes."

A couple of the men nearest the door edged to it and disappeared. The silence was complete except for the squeaking of one of the doors as it swung back and forth. Jaime said sharply to the man nearest the door, "Dolan, bring 'em back."

Dolan, an undersized, sharp-faced man who clerked in the general store, disappeared through the door. Jaime heard him yell. He waited a moment, then crossed to the door himself. Dolan stood a dozen yards away arguing with the two.

"Get back in here, the three of you," Jaime said.

They hesitated. One said something to Dolan in a low tone of voice. The three shuffled toward Jaime sullenly. They went into the saloon and Candelario followed. "Dolan, get yourself a horse and some grub," he said. "Meet me at the jail in twenty minutes. Booker, you do the same. You too, Mansfield."

A man crossed the room from the bar as the three hesitated. "What you're asking isn't right,

144

Sheriff," he said. "You're the one who let things get out of hand by failing to take Clint Morgan into custody. Now you expect us to get you out of the mess you're in."

There was a murmur of agreement within the smoky room. Jaime stared at the man who had spoken, tall, graying, sober of face and eye. "Are you advising these three to break the law, Mr. McCracken?" Jaime said levelly.

"I'm advising them to refuse to be on your posse."

"And I'm telling you to go with them. Get a horse and some grub and meet me at the jail in twenty minutes. That's official, Mr. McCracken. If you refuse, I'll bring charges against you. And against anyone else who balks."

McCracken was silent a moment, his eyes thoughtful. At last he shook his head. "Bring your charges, Sheriff. Maybe the whole conduct of the sheriff's office needs looking into. There are folks who say you're Clint Morgan's man, that you'll wink at anything he does, even at murder."

For the second time in as many days, Jaime Candelario felt the bitter taste of failure. Never before had anyone refused to be a member of one of his posses. Never before had anyone criticized the conduct of the sheriff's office. Turning to face the men in the room he said, "I need a dozen men. Not to fight for Clint Morgan but to keep a range war from starting."

Nobody spoke. "Four men are dead," Jaime said. "More are going to be dead if nothing's done."

Still nobody spoke. Jaime shrugged heavily. He considered resigning as sheriff, considered handing McCracken his badge right now. But he didn't do it. As an individual, he would be helpless to do anything. As sheriff, there was a chance, however small the chance had shrunk.

He walked toward the door, feeling defeat like a sour taste in his mouth. He went out, and heard talk begin to buzz immediately inside.

He paused halfway to the sheriff's office and fished for a cigar. He lighted it and puffed thoughtfully. Was he Clint Morgan's man? Had he changed that much?

He'd deliberately let Morgan Lamb get away when he could have stopped him easily. He'd failed to take Clint when Clint didn't even have a gun. Mary wouldn't have shot him, but of course he hadn't been positive it was Mary behind him at the time.

Or had he? In his own mind, at least, he had been sure. He just hadn't believed Clint guilty of Parfet's death. Or of the deaths of Parfet's men. And he'd known how unfairly Clint would be treated if he was brought to trial.

In one respect, McCracken and the others were right. He hadn't conducted the sheriff's office as impartially as he should since this trouble had come up. A sheriff wasn't supposed to concern himself with the guilt or innocence of those accused of crimes. He was supposed to bring them in and leave their guilt or innocence to the courts.

But he'd never run his job that way and he was damned if he was going to start it now. He knew Clint was innocent of murder. He knew Morgan Lamb was too. If he was discredited and forced out of office for doing what he believed was right, then maybe it was time he got out.

He paced steadily back toward his office, scowling and puffing furiously on his cigar. One thing he wasn't going to do. He wasn't going to sit here on his rump while Duffy and his friends were starting a war at Sombrero ranch. He'd go out there and at least do what he could.

With that decided, he wasted no more time. He went out of his office, locking the door behind. He walked along the street to the livery barn at the edge of town.

Felipe was sitting on a bench in front of the stable. His cigar made a spot of glowing light in the darkness. "I need a horse," Jaime said. "Put a halter on Juan's horse and I'll lead him back. Juan will bring yours back the first time he comes to town."

Felipe got up and disappeared into the stable. Jaime saw the light of a lamp moving back into the depths of it. After several minutes the light returned. Felipe blew it out and led two horses outside. Holding the rope of the haltered horse, Jaime mounted and rode away.

He shook his head grimly as he rode. Morgan Lamb's return had been like a match touched to an open keg of powder. The trouble had been here all the time, waiting, but it had been Morgan's return that set it off.

He tried to plan what he would do when he reached Sombrero tomorrow. Duffy and the others most certainly intended to attack it, kill its defenders and burn it to the ground. If they succeeded in killing Clint, it was probable that they'd get away with it. Amnesty had been granted to the participants in the Lincoln County war. Amnesty would be granted to Duffy and the others simply because it was too difficult to bring thirty men to trial. If Clint Morgan was dead. If he wasn't . . . if Jaime could somehow see to it that he survived . . . then things might be different. Duffy and the others would have to answer for their crimes.

Kehoe was the key to the whole business, thought Jaime. If he could get his hands on Kehoe Lamb before the attack took place . . .

He touched spurs to his horse's sides. And rode through the night, steadily northward, toward his brother's place.

The hours dragged slowly past. Dawn touched the eastern sky and the rising sun turned the clouds blood-red. The sun poked its rim above the plain.

It was well up in the sky when Jaime rode into Juan's yard. Ellen was pacing back and forth nervously on the gallery. A plume of smoke rose from the chimney. The corral was empty and Jaime did not see his brother Juan.

He rode to the house and stared uneasily down at Ellen. Juan's wife came to the door, then disappeared again. "Where's Morgan?" Jaime asked. "I thought . . ."

"I *was* with him. We came here for fresh horses and food and he left me here after running all the horses out of the corral. Uncle Juan went after them on foot but he hasn't come back yet."

"Get a saddle," Jaime said. "We'll see if we can find him."

She ran across the yard and got a saddle from the corral fence. She flung the saddle onto the horse Jaime was leading and bridled him. She mounted.

Jaime picked up Juan's tracks and followed them. Ellen followed silently.

In spite of the gravity of the situation, Jaime found himself grinning ruefully. Ellen was furious at Morgan. Juan would be furious at being forced to chase the horses on foot. But Jaime's respect for Morgan Lamb rose with the realization that he had abandoned Ellen simply because he did not want her sharing his danger.

He wondered briefly where Morgan was.

The trail led away into the empty plain. Nearly ten miles from Juan's house they overtook the man. The horses were grouped on a knoll half a mile farther on.

Jaime stopped his horse while Juan climbed up behind. Then he circled around the bunch of horses and started them back toward home.

Every now and then Juan would utter a bitterly angry curse. They arrived at Juan's house and Juan slipped from his uncomfortable seat on Jaime's horse's rump. Jaime and Ellen drove the horses into the corral.

Jaime dismounted. "Let's get a bite to eat and then I want both of you to come with me," he said. "I can't get up a posse and I can't get any troops. Clint Morgan's going to need all the help that he can get."

They ate hastily, then caught fresh horses out of the corral. It was midafternoon when they rode out.

Jaime knew they probably wouldn't reach Sombrero in time. But he hoped they could arrive before Clint Morgan was killed.

# 16

Until now, Morgan had taken most of the things that had happened to him with a certain matter-of-fact acceptance. He had come here because he had no place else to go. All the blood kin he had in the world were here.

Yet now, as he rode, he wondered if he wanted to stay on. And whether staying was the best course for him to take.

He had liked his mother. He had liked Clint, though he hadn't understood him very well. His presence had certainly made things more difficult for them.

Yet he also understood that they didn't want him to leave. Nor did he himself want to leave. The thought of never seeing Ellen again made him feel unexpectedly gloomy.

Besides, the decision didn't have to be made right now. All that was necessary now was that he elude the sheriff, the group of Sombrero's enemies, and Kehoe Lamb. He grinned to himself briefly. Eluding everyone that was looking for him would be task enough.

He faced squarely the probability that he could not successfully elude them all. Sooner or later he was going to be caught. When he was, he would have to fight.

The thing for him to do was to get angry and stay that way. An angry man fought better than one who was not. Nor would getting angry be very hard. All he had to do was dwell on the injustices of the things that had been done to him since his arrival here.

He rode steadily northward, swinging wide of the place he thought Sombrero headquarters would be, traveling watchfully. Sometimes he dozed briefly in his saddle. Once, his wide mouth curved into a slow smile as he thought of how furious Ellen must have been at his leaving her.

He saw cattle occasionally, and sometimes a band of horses galloping along some ridge or grazing quietly in a brushy draw. Once he startled a bunch of antelope, and they raced away. But he saw no men.

Near sundown, he rode over a low ridge and saw, immediately ahead of him, a squat adobe house.

He halted, frowning. He sat there for a long moment, studying the house.

There was a corral that held a single horse. Beside the corral a black buggy stood, its shafts resting on the ground. There were clothes hanging on a clothesline.

Something about the place . . . It came to him suddenly. The clothes on the line were women's clothes. There was nothing anywhere that looked as if it might belong to a man—no saddle hanging on the corral fence. Even the horse in the corral was obviously a buggy horse.

Furthermore, this was not a ranchhouse with the barns and outbuildings necessary for operating it. It was a dwelling only.

He studied it for a moment more, seeing nothing move. He knew he should eat, but he hadn't wanted to build a fire because he knew the smoke could easily be seen. Nor did he want to wait and build one after dark because in darkness a fire could be seen for miles.

Suddenly, as he watched, smoke came from the chimney of the squat adobe house.

He touched his horse's sides with his heels and rode toward it warily. He slid the rifle out of its scabbard and held it across his knees. He rode to the door, waited a moment, then swung to the ground, the rifle in his hands. He glanced around nervously, tied his horse and approached.

He knocked. After a moment the door opened and a woman stood framed in it.

"You alone here, ma'am?" Morgan said.

She did not immediately reply. Then she nodded. "Yes. I'm alone."

"I . . ." Under the steady scrutiny of her calm eyes he felt confused. "I'm hungry. Do you suppose . . . ? I could pay you for a meal."

"That won't be necessary." She stood aside. "Come in, please."

He started to enter, then stopped, all at once

very conscious of how dirty he was. "Is there someplace I could wash?"

"The pump is over there. I'll get you a towel."

He crossed to the pump. He pumped it until water gushed from its spout, then stuck his head under it. He found a piece of soap on a small bench and lathered his face and hands. He worked the pump handle again and rinsed off suds and dirt.

The woman came out and handed him a towel made from a flour sack. He dried his face and hands. "Come in and eat now."

He followed her into the house, puzzled at something elusively familiar about her. He sat down at the table and watched her. It came to him suddenly as she turned and smiled hesitantly at him. In an obscure way she reminded him of his mother.

And even that was puzzling. They didn't look the same. Yet there was a quality of softness in this woman's face very like that which he had noticed in his mother's face.

She worked at the stove for about fifteen minutes, frying meat, potatoes, and eggs. When she brought the food to the table she said, "I'm Jane Redd."

Morgan stood up. "I'm Morgan Lamb, ma'am."

"Yes. I know." She seemed confused and compelled to explain. She added, "You look like . . ." Her face flushed painfully. "I'm sorry. I hope . . ."

"I know I look like him," he said. "Like Clint Morgan, I mean. Do you know him?"

She glanced at him quickly, studied his face then nodded. "Yes. I know him."

"I guess that question was kind of dumb. I guess everybody knows him."

"Yes. Around here they do."

The conversation was stilted, awkward. There was a sudden strain between them that had not been there before.

Impelled by an obscure desire to confide in her, he said, "The sheriff's after me. I'm supposed to have shot Luke Parfet in the back."

She showed no emotion, no fear, no quick surprise. "I didn't do it," he said, "if you're wondering."

"I didn't for a moment think you had. You're Clint's . . ." She stopped and smiled at him apologetically. "That keeps coming up, doesn't it?"

He didn't answer directly. Instead he asked, "What do you think of him? Of Clint, I mean."

She glanced at him quickly, studied his face almost suspiciously. Then she relaxed visibly and said, "He's a fine man. He's a very fine man who doesn't deserve the unhappiness he's had."

"You know him well?"

"Very well, Morgan. And perhaps that's why I feel that I know you too." Her manner changed abruptly. "Please eat, Morgan. It will all get cold."

He sat down again and began to eat hungrily.

155

When he had emptied his plate she refilled it for him and he emptied it a second time.

He felt a strange closeness to Jane Redd, one he did not understand. He had just met her. How could he feel close to her?

She sipped her coffee thoughtfully and finally asked, "Where are you going now?"

"I'm just trying to stay out of sight. I don't know what else to do. Kehoe Lamb tried to kill me night before last. Yesterday Ellen Candelario and I were chased by a bunch of men . . ."

"How many men?" She was instantly concerned.

"Thirty, I suppose."

"Why? Do you know why they were chasing you?"

"I guess because I got away from the sheriff. They think I killed Parfet."

"Where were they? On Sombrero range?"

He nodded, puzzled at her concern.

"Somebody's got to tell Clint," she said.

He stared at her confusedly.

"Thirty men don't ride Sombrero range unless they're planning something," she said. "Go there and tell him about them. He needs you, Morgan, whether you think he does or not."

"Why should he need me? He's got a million acres of land. He's got thousands of cattle."

"Land and cattle don't keep a man from loneliness."

"You sound as though you know him pretty well." He stared at her, seeing the flush that crept up into her face. And suddenly he understood. This house was on Sombrero range. It was obviously not a working ranch. Jane Redd had to live somehow . . .

He felt a growing dislike for Clint Morgan. It had been his mother first. Now it was Jane Redd.

Jane's flush had faded and now her face was white. But her eyes met his steadily. "Yes, Morgan. I know him very well," she murmured. "And I love him very much."

He got up and strode to the door. There, he stopped, hesitated. He remembered the night at the cabin with Ellen, how he had picked her up and . . . If Kehoe hadn't interrupted by taking a shot at them . . .

Clint was human just as Morgan was. He was obviously in love with Morgan's mother. Without turning he said, "I'm sorry. I guess I've got no right to judge."

She didn't reply. He turned his head and saw that she was weeping silently.

He stood there awkwardly for what seemed like a long, long time. At last her weeping stopped and she looked up at him. "It isn't what you think, Morgan," she said softly. "At least with me it isn't."

"Is he in love with you?"

"He needs me, Morgan. But he will never

157

marry me. He will never marry anyone but your mother."

"Then why . . ."

"Do I go on this way?" She smiled faintly through her tears. "I have asked myself the same question many times. I guess it is because I love him enough to take the part of him that is his to give."

"And you're satisfied with that?" he asked incredulously.

"Satisfied? No. I suppose content would be a better word. I know it is all I will ever have and it's so much better than nothing at all."

"What if . . . ?" He stopped.

"If something happens to Kehoe Lamb? Then I will have lost."

Morgan wanted to kick something. He felt a helpless kind of anger—at Clint because Clint had hurt both his mother and Jane Redd—at Jane because she had told him these things and by doing so had involved him in them. He said tightly, "I'd better go."

"Are you sorry I told you all these things?"

He looked at her. He was sorry, but he shook his head. "I'm glad you did. I guess I am anyway. I don't know."

"Where are you going?"

He shrugged. "Someplace they can't find me, I suppose."

"But not back to Sombrero?"

158

He shook his head.

For the first time, she showed a spark of anger. She got up, crossed the room and faced him, brushing impatiently at her tears. "Do you think he's so big he can't be hurt? Do you think he's immortal? Those men who chased you weren't on Sombrero looking for *you*. They just happened to run into you. They were there to attack Clint. And he doesn't have that many men working for him. By now . . ."

Morgan stared at her, for the moment speechless.

She went on furiously, "If you won't warn him, then I will! Get out of the way, so I can go hitch up my buggy horse."

She tried to brush past him, but he caught her arms. "Let me go!" she said fiercely.

Morgan was realizing that he had never thought of Clint as anything but all-powerful. But this woman had. She had seen Clint when his guard was down, when he was only a man with a man's needs and troubles and uncertainties.

"All right, I'll go," he said.

"Then hurry up and go! You may already be too late."

He released her, turned and stepped outside. He untied his horse.

She watched him from the doorway as he swung astride. "Be careful, Morgan," she said softly. "Be careful of yourself."

"Sure." There were many things he wanted to say to her but suddenly he couldn't say anything. He wheeled his horse and rode away.

The sun was setting. In an hour it would be down. Before he could reach Sombrero it would be dark.

He glanced back once and saw her standing, watching him. Then he went over a low ridge and the small adobe house was lost to sight.

He drummed his heels against the horse's sides, forcing him into a steady lope. He realized how hard it must be for her, alone, wondering if Clint was safe, forced to rely on someone else to do what she so desperately wanted to do herself.

He wasn't even sure he wouldn't miss Sombrero headquarters in the dark but there had to be a road of some kind between Sombrero and Jane Redd's house. Or at least a trail.

He quartered to the left, studying the ground carefully as he rode. He was about to turn back and try the other direction when he discovered it.

It wasn't much of a road. It was more like a horseback trail. Yet there were wagon and buggy tracks and if he was careful he thought he could follow it.

He turned into it, holding his horse to a steady lope.

Thinking of Clint, Morgan was, for the first time since coming here, vaguely ashamed. He'd thought chiefly of himself so far. He hadn't given much thought to Clint. He hadn't considered how hard everything that had happened must be on Clint.

And with Kehoe running loose . . . Clint didn't even dare leave Sombrero because he didn't dare leave Mary Lamb alone.

Morgan was glad he had happened onto Jane Redd's house. He was glad he hadn't left the country. He suddenly wanted to be a part of whatever happened here. Because in a way it was all his fault. His coming had started things.

The sun went down deliberately and the sky flamed orange. Morgan urged his horse on recklessly, slowing him only occasionally when he momentarily lost the road.

# 17

For a long time, Jane Redd stood before her small adobe house, shading her eyes against the sun with an upraised hand and staring after Morgan Lamb. She saw him climb a low rise and disappear beyond it. Even then she did not move, but continued to stare at the place he had disappeared.

Fear was like a cold hand closed around her heart, constricting its beating, making her chest feel tight and painful. At last she lowered her hand and turned.

She hesitated on the gallery, glanced at the buggy horse in the corral and away again. She put a hand on the door . . .

Her thoughts were like flashes of lightning in a sky filled with summer rain. Life had never been easy for her, yet she had never thought of it as being hard. She seldom thought about her lot in life at all. She simply accepted the things that happened because there was nothing to do but accept them. They could not be changed. She was forty-two, and this was the first time she had really been in love.

Not that there hadn't been men in her life. Starting when she was fourteen, there had always been a man in her life. One had died. She had run away from two. One had abandoned her, one she had married when she was twenty-eight, the one named Oliver Redd. She had been thirty-five the day he mounted his horse and headed for town, never to return.

She worked the ranch he left her by herself. Until one day Luke Parfet rode in and stayed to help her with the chores.

She wasn't proud of her association with Luke. He was sometimes brutal toward her, and she was sure he had never loved her. Nor had she loved him. Yet each gave something to the other. She gave Luke the softness, the understanding he never received from his wife. He gave her companionship of a sort, and the help she had to have to survive on her tiny ranch.

But the day Clint Morgan rode in with a roundup crew, all that had changed. Her face softened as she thought of it, of the way he had looked sitting like a giant on his horse, knees gripping the horse's barrel, reins held negligently in his hand. He had seemed a part of his horse that day, as though he were some kind of centaur who used the horse's legs as his own.

He hadn't said a dozen words to her. Yet something had flowed between them, some current of understanding, of need, of hunger perhaps. And she had known he would return.

He did return, of course. And Jane could not have resisted him even if she had wanted to.

He was a ruthless man, truly a giant, who took what he wanted, from people, from life, from the land itself. But he had done more than take, with Jane. He had given too. By needing her so desperately, he had given her the things she needed for herself. And he had talked to her, something no man had ever done before. He had told her about Mary Lamb, about Kehoe, and about Morgan, his son, who was growing up in Illinois. He had needed her physically, for he was a virile man. But he had needed her spiritually too, and for that she had loved him more each day.

When they were together it was like a holocaust. There was violence in it, and there was pain. But there was also deep fulfillment at the end, and a peace such as Jane had never known before.

She whirled suddenly and ran toward the corral as fast as she could run. The buggy horse, normally a placid beast, shied from her as she tried to get a rope on him.

She got the rope on and led him to the buggy. She backed him between the shafts and harnessed him with trembling hands. Then she climbed to the seat, picked up the reins and drove out in the direction of Sombrero ranch. Clint Morgan might die tonight. But if he did, Jane Redd would also die.

She drove recklessly, forcing the horse to run by using the buggy whip. She took turns without slowing. The buggy bounded over the rutted, two-track road like a jack rabbit bounding through the brush.

Her face was intent, her lips compressed. Only her eyes betrayed her fear.

She was a woman, but she had lived most of her life on the prairie. She could read tracks if they were plain enough. She could read the tracks where someone had intercepted Morgan and gone on with him.

It had to have been Clint, she reasoned, else Morgan would have fled from him. And he'd apparently made no attempt to flee.

Relief flooded her, relief so great it made her feel weak and faint. At least Clint was still alive.

His men were with him and so was his son. His enemies had not attacked . . . not yet at least.

The sun touched its golden rim to the western plain. It began to sink slowly out of sight. Jane watched it almost fascinatedly. The setting sun was symbolic today. It was like Clint Morgan, whose influence was also dimming, sinking like the sun into the endless plain.

Kehoe was to blame. Kehoe's hatred had brought all this about. But it was Clint's love for Mary Lamb that had started Kehoe's hatred burning so many years before.

She suddenly wanted to hate Mary Lamb, for holding his affections all these many years, for keeping him and yet giving him nothing in return. But she couldn't hate because she understood. Circumstances might keep her from having Clint, but she would never stop loving him. In that respect, at least, she and Mary Lamb were just alike.

The distance between her small adobe house and Sombrero seemed endless tonight. She fixed her eyes on the land ahead, straining them to see—anything—a plume of smoke, the outline of a building or a tree. She saw nothing. The sun went out of sight, leaving its afterglow on the puffy clouds both to the east and to the west.

Those in the east faded first, and turned dark gray. Afterward, those in the west faded to shades of purple and at last turned gray too.

Still nothing showed ahead. Her buggy whip snaked out and the tiring horse put forth a final burst of speed.

She heard the pound of hoofs above the racket of the bouncing buggy, above the drum of her own horse's hoofs against the ground. She turned her head . . .

Men were overtaking her, spreading as they reached the buggy, coming up on both sides of her. Though she knew it would do no good, she laid the buggy whip against her horse's rump desperately.

A hand caught the horse's bridle, and the horseman slowed his plunging horse and with him the buggy horse. The buggy ground to a halt. Horsemen surrounded her, all but faceless in the darkness, but one she recognized, Nate Duffy, because he was closest to her and because he spoke.

"Where you goin', Miz Redd?"

"You know where I'm going."

"Why you goin' there? You figger on bein' with him when he dies?"

Anger touched her, not so much at the words as at the underlying suggestiveness of his tone. "It won't be him that dies," she said. "It will be you and those with you, once he knows you're here . . ." She stopped, but knew instantly she had stopped too late.

Nate Duffy chuckled. "He ain't goin' to hear

that from you because you ain't goin' no place. You're comin' along with us."

Helplessly she watched as the man who had caught her horse's bridle turned him off the road. Helplessly she sat the buggy seat as they traveled half a mile across country at right angles to it.

They had seen her, she supposed, before the light faded from the sky. They had probably seen Clint too, but hadn't attacked because of the men with him.

She turned her head, counting them in the almost complete darkness. She got to twenty-five but she knew there must be more than that. Why hadn't they attacked Clint a few minutes before, she wondered confusedly. They obviously outnumbered Sombrero's crew. Why had they held back, thus giving Clint an opportunity to get back to Sombrero where his chances would be improved?

"Just as well get down, Miz Redd," Duffy said. "We'll turn you loose in a little bit—soon as we start out."

She climbed to the ground. They hadn't seen Morgan, she realized suddenly, or they wouldn't now be holding her. Neither had they seen Clint. They must have just arrived.

She opened her mouth to tell them that Morgan had undoubtedly already warned Clint of their presence on his range. Then she closed it abruptly. She wouldn't tell them anything. Let them ride in, thinking they had the advantage of surprise. They'd find out they hadn't soon enough.

One of the men called, "How about a fire, Nate? Some coffee and a little grub would sure go good right now."

"Huh-uh. No fires. He doesn't know we're here."

"How do you know? Clint ain't no fool."

"What about the troops the sheriff wired for?" another man said. "They've had time to get here if they started right away."

"Did you ever hear of the Army startin' anything right away? For Christ's sake, quit worrying!"

"Well I am worrying. What if we run head-on into a goddam troop of cavalry?"

Nate's voice was exasperated. "Maybe the whole bunch of you had better quit bellyaching and think about the slice of Sombrero range you're going to get when Clint Morgan ain't around no more. If you're too chicken-livered to fight for a piece of it, then go on back to town. There'll be that much more for the ones who stay."

There was grumbling among the men farthest from Duffy. Jane couldn't make out all their words, but she did catch enough to understand that they were extremely uneasy about what they were going to do. Somewhere out in the darkness she heard a man vomiting. Another, closer, had a bottle. She could hear the liquor gurgling as he poured it down his throat, and afterward heard him cough.

If Clint knew . . . If he knew how much disunion, how much fear and uncertainty was present in these men . . . it might materially affect the outcome of the fight. If she could get away . . . If somehow she could get one of their horses and get away . . .

Duffy didn't seem to be aware of her. He was too concerned with the complaining and uneasiness among his men. "Damn it, Luke Parfet was one of us," he yelled. "You all knew him."

She edged away toward one of their horses standing alone just beyond the buggy. The horse saw her coming and edged away, not used to women or to women's skirts. She followed, and at last managed to catch the horse's reins.

Duffy was still haranguing his men, trying to whip up their anger, trying to bring to the group some kind of unity. She raised her left foot and put it into the stirrup.

She swung astride, hampered by her skirt which billowed out as she did.

The horse shied and got his head down. He began to buck . . .

Jane pulled up his head, using all the strength in both arms before she succeeded in doing so. He stopped bucking and whirled. She loosened the reins slightly and pointed him south.

Behind her, a man yelled surprisedly. Another shouted, "That damned woman of Clint's is gettin' away . . . !"

Half a dozen shots racketed. "No!" Duffy yelled. "Don't shoot at her! Go after her!"

Something like a mule's kick struck Jane in the back. She felt herself falling . . .

The impact of striking the ground knocked the breath from her. She lay spread out, and heard them approaching with running feet. She saw the dark shapes of the men as they gathered around . . .

She felt no fear and no concern about herself. What she did feel was bitter disappointment that she had failed. Now Clint couldn't know the disunion in the ranks of his enemies. This advantage would be denied him at a time when he needed every advantage he could get.

The stars seemed to be fading. The shocked whispers of the men gathered above her seemed to be fading too. She closed her eyes and remembered the last time Clint had come to her . . . Her mouth curved into a gentle smile.

The men above her didn't see the smile. Neither did they see it fade as death relaxed the muscles of her face.

Duffy knelt and seized her wrist. He held it for a long, long time. When he rose, his voice was tight with wrath. "You dumb sons-of-bitches! You goddam stupid fools! You've killed her!"

There was no sound for a long time after that. Then Duffy roared, "You're in it now, the whole damned bunch of you, whether you like it or not! The only chance any of us has got is to see to it Clint Morgan dies before he knows about this."

"What're we goin' to do with her? We can't just leave her here."

"Put her in her buggy. Tie up the reins and turn the damn horse loose. He'll take her home."

They lifted Jane and placed her in the buggy, half-lying across the seat as though she had died right there. They tied up the horse's reins. One of them cut the animal across the rump with the ends of his reins and the horse trotted away with the buggy bouncing along behind.

Duffy stared at them, made uneasy by their silence, by the sudden way they had stopped complaining. He knew, if none of the others did, that unless Clint Morgan died tonight his own life wasn't worth a damn. He hadn't shot Jane Redd, but he would pay the penalty anyway.

# 18

There was a hollow feeling in Duffy's chest as the sounds of the buggy died away. He could feel his hands trembling. A man coughed uneasily.

Duffy wanted to yell at them, wanted to curse them for their stupidity. It hadn't been necessary to shoot Jane. They could have caught her easily. The trouble was, they were all so scared of Clint . . . not one of them was thinking straight.

Maybe he'd been a fool for bringing them out here in the first place. He found himself thinking of Clint, picturing the man in his mind. He admitted something to himself he didn't like having to admit. He was also scared of Clint. Even more scared than he had been before. Clint would be furious when he heard that Jane was dead. He'd know who was responsible.

The law . . . Duffy's mouth twisted. The law couldn't protect him from Clint. Nothing could protect him from Clint. The only way he could go on living was to see that Clint was killed.

The men were stirring uneasily. One of them said, "I don't know about this, Duffy. I think maybe . . ."

Duffy didn't let him finish. It turned him cold to think of them abandoning this attack, dispersing, leaving him to face Clint's wrath alone. "Well I know about it!" he shouted angrily. "What the hell did you think you were coming out here for anyway? Did you think Clint Morgan was going to scare? No, by God! You came out here to fight him. You all knew damned well that unless he was dead you didn't have a chance of getting your hands on part of his range. So what's changed? Jane's dead but nobody can prove any of us did it. If we get Clint, we'll be in the clear.

He's the only one who won't need proof. But if you let him live . . . He'll find out who every one of you is. You won't talk him out of it, either. You *know* what he'll do."

He stopped, breathing heavily, sweating even though the night was cool. Then he went on: "We got more men than he has. There's twenty-seven of us. Clint can't raise over twenty to save his life."

They still were not convinced. Their silence was unnerving. "Damn you," Duffy yelled, "if you run out on me now, I'll see to it that Clint gets a list of names. *I* didn't shoot Jane. I'll leave it to Clint to find the one who did."

At least they weren't silent any more. There was grumbling among them, resentful, angry grumbling. Finally someone said, "All right. Suppose we do go through with it? You got a plan?"

"Plan? You didn't need a plan when you rode away from town. All you could see then was that slice of Sombrero that each of you wanted for yourself."

"Yeah, but . . ."

"All right. I've got a plan. We'll burn 'em out. They've got a whole village of 'dobe shacks outside the wall. When Clint's men see everything they've got going up in flames . . . Which are they going to do, fight us or try and save as much as they can?"

The grumbling continued, but it had a different tone, one of grudging approval. "It might work. It might," one man said.

"Then let's find out."

"Wait a minute!" This was Joe Barth, who lived about a mile from Duffy's place. "Count me out. I didn't shoot Jane and I'm damned if I'm going any further with this."

Duffy had a sudden vision of himself, left with only the half-dozen men who *had* fired at Jane. His chest still felt empty, but it was icy now. He stared in the direction from which Joe Barth's voice had come.

He didn't dare hesitate. He didn't dare give them time to think about what Joe had said. He lunged toward Barth . . .

He reached the man, squat, heavyset, who in darkness reminded him vaguely of Luke Parfet. His hand snatched out his gun. This wasn't going to be a fight. He didn't dare let it be. It had to be over before anyone had time to side with Barth.

He cut at Barth savagely with the gunbarrel. It raked across Joe's face and he staggered back. He snatched out his own gun . . .

Duffy heard the hammer click as it came back. He swung his gun a second time . . .

This time the long barrel struck Barth squarely on the top of the head. It had a solid, sickening sound and Barth dropped without a sound.

Duffy dropped on top of him. Again and again

174

his gun raised and again and again came down until each blow had a wet, bloody, smacking sound. Someone yelled, "Nate! For Christ's sake . . . !"

Sanity was slow returning to him. He stared down at his gun, poised for yet another blow. He couldn't see it but he knew both the gun and his hand were covered with blood. He could feel its wet stickiness.

He stumbled to his feet, shocked at himself, shocked at what he had done. And sick with fear.

Like a cornered wolf he whirled on the others. He was breathing hard and his words came out in breathless gusts. "You bastards . . . you started this just as much as me . . . anyone else that backs out will get what I just gave Joe . . . Now get on your goddam horses and let's go. Or do I have to beat someone else?"

No one said a word. No one made a sound. Like cowed and frightened children they mounted their horses.

Duffy wiped the gun on his pants leg. He shoved it into its holster at his side. He wiped the palm of his hand similarly, but it did not come clean. It had a sticky feeling that would not go away.

He stumbled to his horse and swung astride. He stood up in his stirrups and yelled, "Let's go!"

He rode out at a steady gallop and the others

swept silently along behind. But there was no enthusiasm in Nate.

All this had started as indignation over the deaths of Parfet and his men. It had gone from there to a fight for loot, for a share in the rich acres belonging to Clint. Now it had changed again. Now it had turned into a fight for survival. For only if Clint Morgan was dead could any of them hope to escape responsibility for Jane Redd's death.

And only if Clint was dead could Duffy hope to escape the penalty for killing Barth. With Clint dead and unable to deny the charge, Barth's death could be blamed on him and on his men.

Yet reasoning, this frantic kind of reasoning at least, could not drive away Nate's fear. He was cold with it, numb with it. He was like a stray dog, unexpectedly hurt unbearably. He would strike out at anyone who came close to him no matter who it was.

Waiting was hard for Clint. Waiting for someone else to take the initiative was doubly hard. Yet that was about all he had done so far except for refusing to let the sheriff take him into custody the night before. And it was about all he could do now, at least until one of his riders cut Kehoe's trail.

They had been out all day, scouring the land in all directions from headquarters. Tonight they had come in, singly and in pairs, but none had cut the trail of Kehoe Lamb.

"He's holed up," thought Clint. "He's not making trail."

It was the only explanation. Unless one of the men had missed the trail as he crossed it and that didn't seem likely at all.

He had his supper alone, as usual, then went out onto the gallery to smoke. He puffed thoughtfully on one of his black, Mexican cigars. He had hoped Mary might come out but she did not. After a while he turned to go inside.

He heard the distant drum of hoofs as he put his hand on the door handle. He stopped abruptly and cocked his head, listening.

A single horse. He relaxed. A few moments later a single rider entered the courtyard.

It was Ricardo Perez, who had married one of Pete Candelario's sisters and who now had eleven children. "Señor Morgan?" he called.

"Over here."

Ricardo swung from his lathered horse. "I have found trails, señor. Many trails. Thirty men as nearly as I can tell."

Clint didn't reply. After a moment Perez went on. "They were approaching this place, señor, when I first picked up their trail. They came as close as Little Alkali Wash. There, they came upon two riders and gave chase. I followed for a little while before I came back here."

Clint frowned. It didn't take much astuteness to guess who the thirty were. Sombrero's neighbors, heading for Sombrero to attack. Had they constituted a regular posse, all thirty would not have pursued the pair they had encountered so unexpectedly. Jaime Candelario, had he been with them, would have had more sense.

Nor was it hard to guess who the fugitives were. Morgan and Ellen Candelario.

Little Alkali Wash was about four hours from here. If he left within the next hour, he'd arrive there just as it began to get light. "Find Pete," he said decisively. "Tell him to leave six men here. I want all the others ready to ride in an hour."

"*Si,* señor." Perez mounted his horse and clattered out of the courtyard.

Clint cursed soundlessly to himself. Thirty men. They'd probably caught Morgan already. Damn them, if they hurt him . . .

His chest felt cold. He glanced toward Mary's door, hoping she hadn't heard. He didn't see her and released a long sigh of relief.

A feeling of foreboding touched him. He knew what they'd do to Morgan if they caught him. They'd hang him from the nearest tree. Or from a wagon tongue if they couldn't find a tree. They still remembered his treatment of the horse thieves he'd caught a number of years before. They'd think it symbolic if they gave the same treatment to his son.

He paced furiously back and forth along the gallery, chafing at the enforced delay. It would be better when he got a horse between his knees. At least then he'd be doing something.

Time dragged, but at last he heard them coming. Pete Candelario was leading a saddled horse. Clint saw Mary's door open and saw her come outside, but he didn't speak to her.

He mounted and led out at a steady lope. Pete ranged up beside him and Clint yelled, "How many have we got?"

"Fourteen, counting you and me. I left six behind."

Clint scowled angrily. Fourteen wasn't enough. Not against thirty. Nor were the six he had left behind enough to guard the place in case the raiders got there before he got back.

The trail Perez had found must be almost a day and a night old by now. Yet he knew he couldn't do anything but follow it. He had no other choice. He couldn't ignore the fact that Morgan was running for his life.

The hours dragged maddeningly. At last, as gray was beginning to touch the sky, they reached the place. Perez led them to the trail.

Clint wasted no time studying it. But, when he came to the place where it turned in pursuit of the two fugitives, he took a moment to backtrack the pair.

Their trail had been approaching Sombrero

and this gave him a warm feeling of satisfaction. Morgan had been coming home.

He returned to the main trail and stepped up his pace. The fourteen riders swept along in the increasing light, grim, intent, but angry too. That anyone would dare attack Sombrero angered each of them. That they would dare pursue Clint Morgan's son angered them even more.

Clint glanced at their faces, one by one. His neighbors might hate him, but he commanded loyalty here. He'd seen no fear in any of the faces his glance had touched. Only determination.

The sun was not far above the horizon when they reached the wash in which Ellen and Morgan had stopped to fire at the group. Two dead horses lay bloating on the ground. Clint read their brands.

One belonged to Rufus Latham, whose ranch bordered Parfet's on one side. The other was Link Todd's.

Clint smiled grimly as he continued along the trail. Ellen was smart, all right. She'd bought them a lead of several miles with this little ruse. But he still couldn't be sure it had been enough.

He went on, smiling occasionally at Ellen's strategy. Yet mingling with his satisfaction that Ellen and Morgan were staying ahead of their pursuers was worry at having left Sombrero with so little defense. Half a dozen times he hesitated, on the point of going back, but each time concern for Morgan drove him on. One of their horses could have given out or gone lame. He might, he knew, come upon the place where they'd been caught at any time.

Besides, Clint was realizing something today, something he had never fully realized before. Sombrero meant nothing to him when compared to Morgan's safety. Morgan and Mary were all that really mattered to him.

The sun climbed slowly across the sky. In mid-morning, he found the spot where the pursuers had given up at dark.

He glanced at his horse and at the horses of his men. Most of them were lathered. All showed the effects of the pace he had maintained. They wouldn't make it back to Sombrero as quickly as they had made it here.

He dismounted, frowning, and motioned for his men to do the same. He removed his saddle and began to rub his horse down with the saddle blanket. When he had finished, he lighted a cigar and paced impatiently back and forth. A rest for the horses now would cut time off the journey back. But he chafed at the delay.

He gave the horses half an hour to rest, trying all the while to decide what he should do, hesitating between following the illegal posse or returning to Sombrero immediately. Finally, as he remounted, he decided to follow the group for a little while.

Their trail headed toward Sombrero head-quarters anyway, he discovered. Little time would be lost following them.

At the place the group had camped for the night, Clint stopped his men. Nodding at Pete to accompany him, he rode through the campsite, studying the ground carefully. "Looks like they spent half the night wrangling about something or other," Pete said.

Clint nodded. He noticed two empty whisky bottles lying on the ground. He noticed a place where one man had been sick.

They must have been drunk, at least a few of them had, when they left town. Now they were sobering up and not feeling very good. Added to their headaches was chagrin over their failure to catch Morgan.

Some of them were, no doubt, losing their eagerness to attack. But he was not foolish enough to hope they would all give up. Enough would be left to give him all the trouble he could manage.

Besides, there was still Kehoe Lamb. He hadn't left the country. He was wanted for murder and probably figured that now he had nothing more to lose.

Clint returned to the group, and they continued along the trail, which now began to angle slightly north.

The sun climbed steadily across the sky.

Another hour passed. Then Clint found where the posse had stopped again, briefly, and here, apparently, another argument had occurred. The tracks of two horses broke away from the bunch and headed toward San Juan.

The main trail continued, still angling north. Near noon, Pete Candelario said suddenly, "Señor. Look."

Clint stared in the direction he was pointing. He saw two specks in the distance ahead, specks that were immediately recognizable as men afoot.

He kicked his lagging horse into a trot. Twenty minutes later they reached the pair, who stood watching with their legs spread defiantly.

One was Rufus Latham. The other was Link Todd. They had apparently been riding double since their horses had been killed the day before.

"How many in that bunch you were with?" Clint asked harshly.

Neither man spoke. Pete took down his rope and began to shake out a loop. He said softly, "I'd answer if I was you."

Link spat. But Rufe said sullenly, "There's twenty-seven now. You got that many to fight 'em off?"

Clint didn't reply. Plainly the posse's horses were getting tired or they wouldn't have refused to carry these two double any more. There was obviously dissention in the group.

He nodded curtly at Pete. "Let's go."

183

He circled the pair and went on, abandoning the posse's trail. They wouldn't attack Sombrero today. They'd at least wait until dark when their losses would be less. They'd probably get fairly close and then give their horses the remainder of the day to rest.

He was well north of the home place. North by half a dozen miles. Since a direct line between here and ranch headquarters would take them over several good-sized mesas, he headed for the road leading to Jane Redd's place.

The sun sank steadily toward the horizon. It was going to be close, Clint thought. He couldn't possibly arrive at Sombrero before dusk. And if the raiders attacked at dark . . .

He stepped up his pace, forcing his weary horse into a steady trot. Just after sundown, he reached the narrow road.

The tracks of a single horse were plain in it. And it was not Jane's horse. Its hoofs were too small for that.

He glanced at Pete. "How old?"

Pete dismounted and knelt. "Fresh. Ten minutes maybe."

"Morgan?"

"Or Kehoe Lamb."

"Let's go." He spurred his horse recklessly, knowing it was more likely that Kehoe had made the trail than that Morgan had. And if Kehoe was headed for Sombrero . . .

One of the horses behind him stumbled and fell, throwing his rider clear. Clint did not even look around. He spurred his own horse mercilessly and began to forge ahead of his men.

He crested a low rise suddenly. He saw a single rider ahead.

Unmistakable, even in the fading light. It was Morgan. It was his son.

His breath sighed out involuntarily. He felt almost weak with relief. "Morgan!" he bawled.

Morgan halted his horse. Several minutes later Clint caught up.

He stared at Morgan for a moment, scowling to hide his intense relief. "Looks like you gave 'em the slip."

Morgan nodded. "Ellen did."

"Where is she now?"

"At Juan's place."

"You been at Jane's?"

Morgan nodded.

Clint said heavily, "You're finding a lot of things to hate me for. You hate me for that too?"

For a moment Morgan didn't reply. Then he said slowly, "I suppose I did until I talked to her. I guess I don't any more."

"Seen any sign of Kehoe?" Clint still didn't look at him.

"Couple of nights ago. The night I got away

185

from the sheriff. He took a couple of shots at me."

Clint froze. "Did he . . . ? Do you think he knew who you were?"

"He must have. He followed us all afternoon. He must have gotten a dozen good looks at us."

The men caught up with Clint. One was riding double with Pete. "Were you going home?" Clint asked.

Morgan's eyes met his, and they held a faint surprise. He nodded.

"Then let's get going," Clint said.

He spurred his horse into a trot, and Morgan rode abreast of him. "What happened?" Clint asked. "What made Kehoe give up?"

"I nicked him. Or at least I think I did."

Silently Clint cursed his worn-out horse. No telling what Kehoe might do—or might have already done. Wounded, he would be as dangerous, as unpredictable as a wounded mountain lion.

Clint tried to put himself in Kehoe's place. The thing Kehoe wanted most, he realized, was to hurt him. And what was the thing that would hurt him most?

Mary. God! If Kehoe hurt Mary . . .

He dug spurs savagely into his horse's sides. The animal faltered and nearly fell. Clint forced him on, his mind sick, the ice inside his chest spreading, chilling him . . . Mary . . .

And then, at last, he saw the buildings of Sombrero headquarters ahead of him.

The sky was now almost wholly dark. Clint's horse fell fifty yards short of the courtyard gate. Morgan rode on . . .

Just as he entered the gate, Clint heard a rifle shot, flat and wicked-sounding in the night. He saw Morgan's horse fall . . .

He got up and began to run. He seized Morgan and dragged him back out the gate as the rifle spat again.

Morgan was cursing, softly, angrily. "Where'd he hit you?" Clint asked. "Is it bad?"

Morgan stopped cursing. "In the leg. It burns like hell but I don't think it's very bad."

Pete Candelario ran up. "It's Kehoe," Clint said. "He's in the house. Tell the men to surround the place. Don't let him get away."

Pete moved away in the darkness. Clint heard him giving orders to the men.

But he knew Kehoe wouldn't try to get away. At least not yet. Not until he had finished what he had come here to do.

He fished a cigar from his pocket and struck a match against the wall. The rifle spat again. The bullet struck the ground beyond the gate and whined away into the night.

"What does he want?" Morgan asked. "He must be crazy coming here like this."

Clint nodded. Kehoe was crazy all right. The

years of hatred and bitterness had at last become too much for him. And Clint knew what he wanted now. Kehoe would not be satisfied until he, Morgan, and Mary all were dead.

# 19

All day Kehoe Lamb rode, from the place he had stopped to dress his wound, northward in an effort to cut Morgan's and Ellen's trail. He was weak, and sick, and there were times when he dozed in the saddle in spite of himself.

Perhaps he missed their trail because Ellen had hidden it so skillfully. Or perhaps he missed it during one of his short periods of sleep. But by the time the sun started down the western sky, he knew he had crossed it without seeing it. Or that Morgan and Ellen had gone the other way.

He halted his horse. He was sweating heavily, both from weakness and from pain. He wanted to dismount, to lie down and rest but he would not permit himself this luxury. There wasn't time. He was hunted and it was only a matter of time until he would be caught. What he had to do must be done before he was.

Morgan was lost to him. He had failed last night in his attempt to kill Morgan. But there was still Clint. And there was Mary . . .

If he could get back to Sombrero . . . If he

could get into the house without being seen . . .
A bitter smile touched his long, thin mouth. What
better way to hurt Clint than to kill Mary right
in front of him? And then, when that was done,
kill Clint himself? Only he wouldn't kill Clint
quickly. He'd draw it out and make it last. He'd
cut Clint's legs out from under him and make
him crawl . . . He'd put each bullet into a place
where it would hurt but wouldn't kill.

His thoughts of revenge sent new strength
coursing through his veins. He felt a rising
excitement in spite of his weakness and his
wound. He turned the horse's head slightly
westward and headed straight for Sombrero
headquarters.

The sun sank slowly ahead of him. It burned
mercilessly into his face. He rode more watchfully now, aware that the closer he got the greater
his danger would be.

He ought to wait for dark, he thought. He ought
to hole up someplace and go in when his chances
were greatest to succeed.

But he couldn't wait. The more he thought of
finally obtaining revenge for the past twenty
years, the less he was able to put it off.

He knew this land, knew every knoll, every
small draw deep enough to conceal a man and
horse. And he took advantage of every bit of
cover available.

Ultimately, he reached a spot from which he

could see the house without being seen. Here, he dismounted and tied his horse. He slipped his rifle from the saddle scabbard and carrying it, inched his way forward.

He stopped and watched the house steadily for almost an hour. He saw women moving about among the adobe huts. He saw children playing. He saw the six men Clint had left behind clustered in a group at the courtyard gate, smoking, talking among themselves.

Of Clint Morgan himself he saw nothing. Nor did he see Mary Lamb.

He retreated at last and, afoot, circled around until he was behind the house. From this spot he watched for another ten minutes until he was sure no one was guarding this approach. Then, bending low, he crossed the clear space between himself and the house at a shambling trot.

At the adobe wall of the house he stopped. The sun was almost down. He leaned against the rough wall, his breath coming in gusts. With each breath, his wound throbbed. His knees trembled with weakness.

He cursed his weakness soundlessly. If he passed out now . . .

His teeth clenched. He deliberately fanned his hatred and fury into a white-hot flame. Then, strengthened by their very intensity, he glanced up at the small windows of the house. One of them had to be open. One of them had to be low enough to reach.

And one was. One that opened into the main part of the house, which Clint occupied.

There were bars at the window as there were at all the windows on this side of the house. Bars originally intended to keep marauding Indians out. But the years had loosened them. Standing tall, Kehoe yanked at one corner and was showered with adobe dust.

The bars did not come free. He raised his rifle and, using the barrel as a pry, tore them loose. They clattered to the ground at his feet.

He stood there frozen for several minutes, listening. Then he stooped and picked up the bars. He leaned them against the wall of the house in such a way that they formed a short ladder. He climbed the rungs high enough so that he could look inside.

The room, a bedroom, was empty. Now, if he had strength enough to get inside . . .

He laid his rifle on the wide adobe sill. He reached in as far as he could and got a grip on the sill where the bars had been. He put forth a burst of effort.

For several moments he flopped like a fish out of water, trying to wriggle upward and into the room. He failed, and hung there helplessly while pain mounted to an intolerable pitch in his wounded arm. Sweat sprang from his pores.

He thought of Clint, who would win if he failed in this. He thought of Mary, of her betrayal, and he thought of Morgan, the living evidence of that betrayal.

He tried again, kicking violently with his feet, pulling with both arms, trying to ignore the pain in the wounded one.

It began to bleed profusely, making the window sill slick with blood. But suddenly he was balanced on the sill, and from there on it was easy. He flopped inside the room, prone, and his rifle clattered down to the floor at his side.

Seizing it, he rolled to face the door. He laid there still for several minutes while his breathing quieted, while a part of his strength returned. When he got painfully to his feet, he left another spot of blood on the floor where he had lain.

Carefully now, he crossed to the door and opened it. He peered out into the hall, relieved to find it empty. He went down the hall and entered the enormous living room, to find it empty too.

Clint must be gone, he thought, and a grim smile touched his mouth. Looking for him. Scouring Sombrero range for him.

He went to the door and opened it a crack. He peered out, seeing the six Clint had left behind still lounging beyond the courtyard gate. They weren't looking at the house. He opened the door a little wider and eased through onto the gallery.

He moved slowly, inch by inch along it toward

Mary's door. It no longer mattered if he was discovered. Before any one of the six could reach him, he would be safely inside.

He had won! In spite of his wound, in spite of Clint Morgan, in spite of everyone, he had won! In another minute, he'd be inside and once he was, once Mary was his prisoner, Clint would do whatever he was told to do.

He reached the door. He opened it slowly and ducked inside, still unseen by the men outside. He turned . . .

Mary stood in the kitchen doorway. There was a gun in her hand. She said in a trembling voice, "Stay right where you are. Don't come any closer to me."

Her eyes widened as she saw the blood that covered him. She put the gun down and crossed the room.

Kehoe struck her with the flat of his hand squarely on the cheek. She staggered away, then whirled and ran for the gun she had just put down.

Kehoe pushed himself away from the wall, extending his rifle before him. He intercepted her and pushed it in front of her running feet.

She stumbled and fell headlong, inches short of the gun. Kehoe picked it up and unloaded it, putting the cartridges in his pocket. He stared down at her.

His eyes were narrowed, both with fury and

with pain. His teeth were set. There was several days' growth of whiskers on his face. He was dusty and rank with stale sweat.

His voice was thin and cold. "Bitch! This is the day you and Clint pay off. For twenty years of my life. For that bastard son of yours. This is the day."

She didn't immediately reply. Her eyes studied him, this man she knew so well, with whom she had lived for twenty years. When her voice did come it was almost calm. "What are you going to do?"

He chuckled softly. "You'd like to know that, wouldn't you? You'd like me to tell you what I'm going to do. Well, I'm not going to tell you yet. I'm going to let you think about it. If you're not sure it'll be worse than if you knew."

"You killed Luke Parfet, didn't you?"

"Sure I did. But I didn't get blamed for it. Clint got blamed. And Morgan. If Morgan gets away from me he'll hang for it."

He wished he hadn't said that, because her eyes lighted up. She hadn't known. She had been afraid he'd hurt or killed her son. He'd done her a favor he hadn't intended when he'd let that slip.

She didn't move. She just kept staring up at him, an unreadable expression in her eyes. "Get up!" he said savagely. "Go out in the kitchen and get me something to eat. I'll watch for Clint."

194

Silently she got to her feet. Silently she went into the kitchen.

Kehoe crossed to the window. He could feel weakness overcoming him and so sat down in a straight-backed chair. He stared into the courtyard, at the six waiting out there at the gate, at the last, long shadows of the setting sun.

He closed his eyes. Weakness flowed through him in waves. He forced his eyes open, forced himself to sit straighter in the chair. He couldn't allow weakness to defeat him, to cheat him of his revenge after all these years.

He had not considered what would happen to him after Clint and Mary were dead. He thought about it now.

He hadn't a chance to escape, he realized. If Sombrero's riders didn't smoke him out and kill him, he'd hang for murder. Clint's and Mary's lives might end tonight, but his would be ending too.

But he didn't care. He'd lived for vengeance almost twenty years. There would be nothing to live on for after tonight, after his thirst for vengeance was satisfied.

The sun was now completely down. Briefly, its last rays stained the mesa tops to eastward and touched the clouds with an orange glow. Then the sky turned gray and dusk crept across the land.

With a part of his mind, he listened to Mary

moving about in the kitchen. He heard all the familiar sounds that accompanied the preparation of a meal. Afterward, he heard her coming and turned his head as she put a plate down on a chair in front of him. "Get back in the kitchen and stay there," he said.

She stood beside him for a moment, looking down. Her face was white and tense with fear. Her eyes looked at him in much the same way she would have looked at a mad dog. With fear. With anxiety for what he might do. But with pity too.

He opened his mouth to snarl at her, but closed it as she turned and silently withdrew.

In the fading light, he began to eat. He didn't want the food and each mouthful made nausea stir in his stomach. He wondered if she had poisoned the food, then dismissed the thought immediately.

He forced the food down, to the last mouthful on the plate. Food would give him the strength he had to have. Food would make possible what he still had to do tonight.

Dimly in the distance, he heard the steady thunder of approaching horses' hoofs. It began as a rumbling in the floor beneath his feet, only becoming an actual sound in the air later when the approaching riders were close.

He straightened and turned away from the food. He peered out the window into the deep gray dusk. He knocked out a pane of window glass and poked the muzzle of the rifle out.

The thunder of hoofs was closer now. And suddenly Kehoe saw a rider wheel his horse into the gate.

The six who had been on guard had straightened beside the gate. They seemed uncertain as to what they ought to do.

That rider who had wheeled into the gate . . . There was something familiar about him even in the dark, even in silhouette. The rider had to be Morgan . . .

Kehoe fired almost instantly. He saw the horse fall, saw the man thrown clear. He drew a bead for another shot . . .

A running figure, afoot, came through the gate, and this one was more easily recognizable to him. It was Clint.

Clint seized the downed rider and dragged him back toward the gate. Kehoe fired again.

This shot missed, perhaps because he had changed his point of aim at the last moment before he squeezed it off. Both Clint and the other disappeared behind the courtyard wall.

Kehoe began to curse softly to himself. He heard Mary behind him and whirled. She had a skillet in her hands, raised above her head.

He swung the rifle barrel instinctively. It struck her and knocked her aside, staggering. The skillet clattered on the floor.

Mary bent double, hugging her stomach. He couldn't see her face because the room was dark. He began to curse her in a monotonous, steady tone.

He turned his head and watched the courtyard gate, the rifle ready. He saw a match flare and fired instantly.

The bullet struck the wall and whined away into the night. Kehoe waited, stronger than he had been before, alert and ready for whatever might appear.

And gleeful too. Because he now was sure he had all three of them. Mary here. Clint and Morgan out there. He had the means to kill them all.

All he had to do was threaten Mary and both Clint and Morgan would do whatever he told them to. He began to chuckle to himself.

It was an eerie sound under the circumstances and it brought a weak moan of protest from Mary. She came to the window beside him.

"They're both out there," he said triumphantly. "Clint and Morgan too."

"Did you . . . ? Are they . . . ?"

"I hit Morgan once. But Clint's all right."

Her voice was the merest whisper. "What are you going to do?"

He began to chuckle again. "I'm going to kill all three of you."

# 20

For several long moments there was complete silence, broken only by the sound of Morgan shifting position to ease his leg. Clint asked immediately, "Is it bleeding much?"

"I don't think so. It's kind of numb."

"Can you walk on it?"

Morgan took two or three hobbling steps. "Uh-huh."

Clint puffed furiously on his cigar. He wanted to take Morgan to one of the adobe houses outside the courtyard wall and get the leg looked after, but he couldn't leave here now.

He stared northward into the darkness. That bunch he'd been trailing might arrive at any time. If they did, things could get damned awkward . . .

"What does he want?" Morgan asked.

"Me, I suppose."

"Couldn't we . . . ? I mean, it's too dark now for him to see anything out here. If we could get through the gate . . ."

"He's with your mother, boy," Clint said. "We don't dare rile him up."

"But we can't just wait."

"We can and will. Until Kehoe decides what it is he wants." But he already knew what Kehoe would want. He'd want all three. And Clint's thoughts were like caged animals, searching for a way he could give Kehoe part of what he demanded and only part. Somehow he had to see to it that Mary lived. And that Morgan did.

It struck him suddenly how powerless he was right now. He'd built a ranch of well over a million acres. He didn't even know how many cattle he had. He could write a check in five figures without worrying much about it. But he couldn't help Mary now when she needed him more than she ever had before.

He knew that he was going to die. Tonight. He would die at Kehoe's hands and there wasn't a thing in the world he could do to change that fact.

He accepted it fatalistically. Yet his thoughts continued to probe the situation almost frantically. Somehow there had to be a way. To give Kehoe only him. To cheat the man of Mary and her son.

A shout broke the stillness suddenly. "Clint!"

Clint stepped to the courtyard gate. Without exposing himself he yelled, "I'm here!"

Kehoe was silent. For several minutes there was no sound from the house.

Clint's mouth twisted. Even now, Kehoe had to turn the knife. He knew what Clint was thinking as well as Clint knew himself. He knew how silence and uncertainty would hurt.

At last he yelled again, "Clint! You still there?"

"I'm here!"

"Get yourself a torch."

There was another long silence, broken at last by the shout, "Morgan!"

Clint whirled and groped for Morgan's arm in the darkness. Too late he whispered hoarsely, "Don't say anything! He isn't sure you're here!" But Morgan had already replied. And over at the house, Kehoe began to laugh.

Clint cursed soundlessly. Kehoe shouted, "So you're both out there! I thought it was Morgan I knocked off that horse!"

Where was Mary, Clint wondered. Was she all right? Or had Kehoe already killed her?

He'd know the answer soon enough. He'd know . . . Or would he know? Would he ever know?

"Get two torches then," Kehoe yelled. "One for each of you."

It was Clint's turn to be silent as he understood what Kehoe had in mind. Kehoe wanted him and Morgan to cross the courtyard carrying torches, so that he could see to shoot. Clint's mouth twisted. He could imagine how this was going to go. No clean shots to end it quickly. Not for Kehoe. That wouldn't adequately satisfy his hate.

He'd place his shots in non-vital spots. He'd break their legs, their arms. He'd cut them to pieces before he killed them.

"You hear me?" Kehoe bawled. "Damn you, Clint, do what I say!"

Clint put a hand on Morgan's arm. "Quiet. Wait."

Because there was something he had to know. If Mary was all right. If she wasn't . . .

"I've got Mary here! You hear me, Clint? You know what I'll do to her if you don't do what I tell you to?"

"And suppose we do?" Clint roared. "What then? Will you let Mary go?" He knew he was making an unenforceable bargain. Kehoe's word to let Mary go would be worthless.

"Tell Pete to have the place surrounded. Tell him not to let me go unless I send Mary out first."

Clint released a long, slow sigh. He wasn't going to get a better bargain than this. In the end, Mary's life would be safe only to the extent that Kehoe valued his own. If he wasn't afraid to die then Mary didn't have a chance.

"I want to see Mary before we do anything," he yelled.

"All right. But you'd better tell the men not to get trigger-happy. I'll have a gun at Mary's head."

Clint turned his head. "Pete?" he called.

"I heard him, Clint. Don't worry about us." The voice was soft, but it was filled with suppressed fury.

"Send somebody for a couple of torches," Clint said. "Tell him not to hurry. We'll stall as long as we can."

He returned his attention to the house. A lamp flickered dimly through the window of the house. The door opened and a shaft of light streamed out, falling on the gallery and on the courtyard beyond. Kehoe pushed Mary into the doorway, holding her with one hand, holding a gun against her head with the other. All that was visible of Kehoe himself were his arms and face.

"Clint!" Mary screamed. "Don't do it! Don't do what he says! He's going to kill you and Morgan. He's going to make me watch and then kill me too!"

She was yanked back savagely and the door slammed. Clint realized that his hands were clenched. The blood was pounding in his head. Never before in his life had he so wanted a man between his hands. Never had he felt this fierce and savage urge to kill.

Kehoe's voice, thick with fury, came again from the open window of the house, "Clint! If you want to see her thrown out the door dead, then stay where you are. If you don't, you'd better get those torches."

"I've sent for them!" Clint roared. All four of them were going to die, if Kehoe had his way. Kehoe knew that the men of Sombrero would never let him go, not after he had killed Clint, not even to save Mary's life. Nothing he could say to them now . . . no order he could give would control their wrath later at his being killed.

Kehoe must also realize this, and be ready to die himself. But before he did he wanted the last full measure of revenge.

"He won't let her go," Morgan whispered. "Not even if we do exactly what he says."

"I know it." There wasn't much chance of upsetting Kehoe's plans. But if he refused to walk out there . . . Kehoe *would* kill Mary and push her body out. Lacking the complete revenge he planned, he would take at least that much.

Light flickered on the outside courtyard wall. Clint turned his head and saw a man approaching from the adobe houses carrying two torches, one in each hand.

And he heard something . . . something he had been hoping desperately he wouldn't hear just yet. The sound of many hoofs, a faint rumble at first but one which grew as the moments passed until it was unmistakable.

There was a flurry of movement . . . Pete Candelario's voice shouted, "Here they come! Scatter! Wait till they get close enough, then dump all of the horses you can!"

Clint didn't move. He glanced at the house, then back at the man with the torches, who was running now. Those torches . . . they'd make perfect targets out of Morgan and himself. As they crossed the courtyard . . . if Kehoe didn't cut them down the bunch of Sombrero's neighbors would.

A flurry of shots racketed, fired by the few overanxious ones in the raiding group. The man carrying the torches dropped them and scurried away into the darkness.

Clint ran to his horse and yanked the rifle from the saddle boot. He levered in a shell, knelt, and as the group thundered into the light of the two torches which lay blazing on the ground, he squeezed his first shot off. Beside him another rifle roared and he turned his head and grinned briefly at his son.

Two horses crashed to the ground, rolling, kicking, throwing their riders nearly twenty feet. The pair got up and scurried into the darkness, one of them limping, dragging a twisted leg.

From the adobe houses, from the shadow of the courtyard wall, from the open darkness between, rifles and revolvers now flashed, pouring a deadly hail into the ranks of the attackers, who had pulled up and who now milled uncertainly in the torches' light.

Two more horses fell. Someone roared at them to get out of the light. They wheeled and swept away at a hard run, disappearing almost instantly.

A voice shouted taunts at them in Spanish. Other voices took it up. "Pete!" Clint yelled. "Tell 'em not to feel too good just because they knocked a few horses off their feet. That bunch will be back again."

Now was the time, he knew. The attackers had

probably not stopped before they were a quarter mile away. Now, he and Morgan would at least be safe from their bullets from behind. They could concentrate on getting across the courtyard, on reaching Kehoe Lamb.

"I'll get the torches," Morgan said. His voice was scared, but it was steady. Clint felt a surge of pride in him.

And he knew something he should have known all along. He wasn't going to let Morgan walk across the courtyard with him. Kehoe could go to hell. He had Clint and Mary exactly where he wanted them but he'd have to be satisfied with the two of them. He wasn't going to get Morgan too.

"Your leg's hurt," he said. "I'll get 'em."

He walked past Morgan, heading in the direction of the torches. And suddenly he turned . . .

He saw realization of what he intended to do in Morgan's startled face. Morgan got out the words, "No! Don't . . ."

Clint's fist took him squarely on the jaw. He staggered back, slammed against the adobe courtyard wall and stood there for an instant, eyes glazing, mouth slack, before he slid slowly to a sitting position at the base of the wall. His head lolled forward . . .

Clint sprinted for the torches, aware that as he did he was exposed to Kehoe's fire from the house. But no shots racketed. There was only silence.

He reached the torches and seized one of them in each hand. Without ever completely stopping, he ran on, turning as he did, circling back toward the courtyard gate. "Clint!" Pete called. "Don't do it! He'll kill Mary anyway!"

He didn't answer that. He reached the wall and beat one of the torches against it. Sparks showered down, but the flame in the torch went out. He flung it, smoldering, into the darkness.

"You coming, Clint?" Kehoe bawled. "You're makin' me edgy with all this goddam waiting! You'd better show up pretty soon!"

"I'm coming!" Holding the torch in his left hand, his revolver in his right, Clint looked down at Morgan, slumped against the wall. Morgan groaned and stirred.

A faint smile touched Clint's hard, seamed face. It had come to this, but he wouldn't do any differently if he had the chance to do it all over again. Mary . . . Morgan . . . He had Mary's love and, he thought, Morgan's respect at least. It was more than many men achieve. It had never seemed enough to live with, but it was enough to die with.

He heard the pounding hoofs again. "Keep 'em off my back, Pete!" he yelled.

Pete's voice sounded as though he were choking. "*Si*, señor. They will not shoot at you."

Clint stepped past Morgan. He paused for an instant in the center of the courtyard gate.

By the light of the torch, he could see the house. He could see Kehoe's white face in the window and beside it, Mary's whiter one. Mary's face was twisted with pain and he realized Kehoe was holding her there by twisting cruelly on her arm.

His fury rose again. Kehoe was going to make her watch. He was going to cut Clint's legs out from under him and make him crawl, and he was going to make Mary watch it while he did.

He had faced danger many times in his life. He had faced death but he had never before accepted the fact that he would die.

He did so now as he began to pace slowly toward the house. A step at a time, and a pause between each one.

His body was more tense, more ready than it had ever been in his life before. Every muscle was taut, every nerve alive. Perhaps his chance would come, and if it did he would be ready to take advantage of it.

He stared steadily at Kehoe's face. It was not, tonight, the face of the man who had ramrodded Sombrero for him all these years. It seemed thin, and gray, and it sometimes seemed to be twisted with pain. Perhaps Morgan *had* wounded him, as he had thought.

Kehoe's eyes burned with a light all their own.

They caught the orange light of the torch and threw it back, the way Clint had sometimes seen an animal's eyes do.

He shifted his glance briefly from Kehoe's face to Mary's. There was pain in her face too, pain from the cruel twisting of her arm. But in her eyes . . . they were bright with unshed tears. And there was so much love . . .

Why couldn't it have been different, he thought. Why couldn't he have found Mary before Kehoe did?

She would wince each time a bullet struck . . . And he didn't dare shoot back. Not with the light as uncertain as it was. Not with Kehoe holding her so close to him.

Behind him the thunder of approaching hoofs grew loud again. Shots cracked like strings of firecrackers exploding on the Fourth of July. A horse nickered and snorted with pain. A man screamed, and screamed, and finally his screams subsided into long, sobbing groans.

It seemed like an hour to Clint since he had left the courtyard gate. It seemed that long, yet he had taken no more than a dozen steps.

And then Mary screamed—like a lost soul. When her scream had died away, her words came almost like a sob, "Clint! Oh God, Clint, please go back. If you love me, please go back!"

Clint heard sound behind him, a shuffling sound like someone running after him, but he didn't dare turn around. He fixed his eyes on Kehoe's face and took another step. Whatever happened would happen. Until it did, he would keep his eyes steadily on Kehoe's face because in doing so lay his only hope.

# 21

The shuffling sound was right beside him now. And from that direction came Morgan's voice, unsteady, but strong enough. "You sure pack a wallop. I'll say that for you."

Without turning his head, Clint said bitterly, "You're a fool! Why didn't you stay where you were?"

"Because this way he's got two of us to watch. And two guns to worry about instead of one."

"Don't shoot at him!" Clint's voice was harsh. "He's got your mother too close."

Behind them, the gunfire dwindled to a spasmodic crackling. A reddish light began to grow on the far side of the house. From behind them came more reddish light, throwing itself against the front wall ahead.

Clint's eyes held a grimly fatalistic quality. Apparently the attackers had split. Some of them had set fire to the house. Others had fired the adobe village where the hands and their families lived.

Kehoe roared with taunting laughter. "They're burning you out, Clint! When they get through with you there won't be a damned thing left but a few adobe walls."

"Get on with it, you son-of-a-bitch!" Clint roared. But he knew how precarious his situation had suddenly become. No one fights well while his home goes up in flames, while his family is endangered. His men were no exception. Without him to direct them they'd abandon the defense of Sombrero and turn their attention to the flames . . .

Still grinning triumphantly, Kehoe raised his gun. He snapped a shot at Clint.

The bullet tore into his left leg. It felt like a mule's kick and had almost the same impact force. It tore his leg out from under him and dumped him face downward in the dirt.

Fury raged in Clint, helpless fury because he could not retaliate. Mary screamed again, wordlessly. Clint struggled to get up, fighting a leg that was numb and drenched with blood, a leg that would not do what his brain told it to.

He rolled onto his side, put his hands down and forced himself up on one knee. Morgan had stopped a pace or so ahead, but so far had not turned his head. Still without turning it, he said, "You're hit, aren't you? How bad . . . ?"

Clint's face was bathed with sweat. His teeth were clenched against the pain that had come on like a flood. He said shortly, "Keep your eye on him. It ain't bad. I just stumbled, that's all."

Kehoe was sighting carefully this time. Clint watched him helplessly, not daring to use his own gun because Mary was still held close . . .

This time, he thought, Kehoe would smash a shoulder or an arm. Then, while Clint's life bled slowly onto the ground, he'd turn his attention to Morgan.

But Clint's gun was up, ready for the chance that might never come. His teeth hurt from the pressure of clenching his jaws. And his anger was towering.

It seemed like an hour that they remained thus, frozen into immobility. Kehoe's gun barrel centered itself on Clint. In another instant it would belch smoke and flame and the bullet would . . .

But suddenly there was movement. He tore his glance briefly from Kehoe's face. A shape moved into his line of vision—Morgan—running, weaving to right and left as he charged directly toward the house.

He couldn't see Morgan's face, but the lines of Morgan's body, his movements were eloquent of his rage. He was a fool. Now Kehoe would cut him down.

He'd have to shoot, but it would have to be carefully. It would have to be the best shooting he had ever done in his life before.

He looked straight at Kehoe again, surprised

to discover that Kehoe's gun was no longer pointing at him. Instead it was trying to follow Morgan's weaving movements . . . And there was something in Kehoe's face, some expression that had not been there before . . .

Mary began to struggle with him. Her face was without color but there was no terror in it any more. Only fury—the determined fury of a woman who has been hurt as much as she can be hurt—as much as she will be hurt.

Kehoe cursed her savagely as her teeth sank into his arm. He flung her away from him, violently, instinctively. He made a swift, determined effort to get Morgan in his sights.

But he stood alone, without a shield, without Mary to hide behind. Clint's gun fired instantly. Morgan, who had stopped running as Kehoe flung Mary away from him, raised his own gun and fired pointblank from a distance of less than fifteen feet . . .

One of the bullets took Kehoe in the throat. It gushed blood instantly. The other struck him squarely in the chest, flinging him back into the darkness beyond the window.

Morgan plunged toward the house. He crossed the gallery and disappeared into the door. "Morgan! Damn it . . . !" Clint roared.

Morgan reappeared. He stared at his father, then turned his head and looked back into the room.

Then, as though having decided something, he thrust his gun into his belt and returned to Clint. He stooped and helped Clint to his feet.

Supporting his father on the left side, he helped him across the gallery to the door. Clint seized the doorjamb with both hands. "I can make it now," he said fiercely.

He went through the door, furious at the leg because it would not support his weight, but unwilling to let Mary see him helpless now.

Kehoe was lying in the center of the room on his back. There was blood on his filthy shirt front and a pool of blood beneath his head. Mary . . . she was over against the wall, slumped, sobbing uncontrollably.

Clint said, "Mary," his voice hoarse but very soft.

Her eyes lifted. For an instant there was shock in them, and unbelief. Then . . . it was like the sunlight streaming through the clouds after a summer storm. It was like a thousand dawns. It was enough to make Clint's throat grow tight, to make him forget his wound, enough to make tears burn his eyes.

Morgan picked up Kehoe's arms and dragged him out the door. Mary scrambled to her feet. She stood there unsteadily for an instant, then ran to Clint. She flung her arms around his neck. "Clint! Clint!"

It was all she could say, his name, and she repeated it over and over again.

He held her, releasing his hold on the doorjamb. With no support he fell helplessly, pulling her to the floor with him.

"Morgan! Morgan! Hurry!" she screamed.

Morgan came in, knelt and shook her shoulders gently. "It's his leg. We need some light and we need some bandages."

They lifted him, the two of them, and helped him to a couch. Morgan lighted another lamp and brought it close while Mary rummaged for bandages.

Through the windows and the open door, Clint could hear the shots still being fired outside. He could see the ominously growing light from the fires. There wasn't going to be much left when this was over, but he didn't care. The three of them were here, together and close, as a family ought to be. For now that was enough.

Morgan cut away his pants leg, dumped whisky over the wound and wiped it clean. Mary wound it with bandages while Morgan held his foot.

He remembered her face, so filled with softness, with concern for him. He remembered a feeling of well-being. He started to rise so that he could go direct the defense of Sombrero from those attacking it.

The room . . . Mary . . . Morgan . . . whirled

briefly before his eyes. Then blackness descended and he knew no more.

Morgan seized his wrist as he fell back. He felt for a pulse, then turned and smiled reassuringly into his mother's worried eyes. "His heart's hammering like it was trying to get out of his chest. He'll be all right. He's just weak from loss of blood."

She did not lift her glance from Clint's face. All its harsh lines had softened and it had lost color. Clint's lips were bluish gray.

In spite of Morgan's reassuring words, her fear for Clint continued. She heard Morgan leave, and raised her eyes. Her lips moved soundlessly as she prayed for both of them.

Outside the spasmodic crackling of gunfire continued. The flames in the brush and sod roofs of the adobe huts made a continuous roar.

She heard Morgan shouting . . . And Clint stirred and groaned softly. Smoke, drifting in through windows and doors made a thin, bluish layer in the upper air of the room. Clint choked, and began to cough.

It wasn't over, she realized. Kehoe no longer threatened them but there were others . . . Morgan was out there right now, in danger. If Clint regained consciousness, he'd want to go out there too.

She looked down at him. His eyes were open,

watching her. She leaned over and touched his lips gently with her own.

"Where's Morgan?" he asked.

"Out there."

"How long . . . ?"

"Just a few minutes. You've only been unconscious a few minutes."

He struggled to sit up, but she pushed him back. "You can't go out. You're too weak from loss of blood."

His eyes met her steadily. "Mary, Morgan is our son. I'm not going to lie here . . ." He struggled again and this time made it to a sitting position. His face lost what little color remained in it and for an instant Mary thought he would lose consciousness again.

But his jaw hardened with determination. He shook his shaggy head. "Help me . . ."

"What do you want me to do?"

"Help me up. Help me get a horse and get on him."

"Clint, please . . . You can't . . ." Her eyes met his, battled with them and lost. She nodded wearily. "All right, Clint." She sat down beside him, put an arm around him and helped him to his feet.

He leaned heavily on her for several moments while he fought his dizziness. Then, determinedly, he took a step toward the door.

Mary walked with him through the door and out

onto the gallery. He released her and put an arm around one of the logs that supported the gallery roof. "Go back in and get me a gun," he said.

She ran into the house and picked up Kehoe's revolver from the floor. She returned and gave it to Clint.

A couple of horses were standing just outside the courtyard gate. Beyond them she could see the blazing adobe huts of the hands. Men, women, and children were running aimlessly around trying, in a disorganized way, to put out the fires.

"See if you can catch one of those horses," he said. "I'll cover you from here."

She ran across the courtyard. "Easy," Clint called. "Don't scare 'em off."

She stopped running and walked, slowly, talking to the horses as she approached. They eyed her skirts and moved away, trailing their reins. She watched them, almost with satisfaction. If she couldn't catch one of them it would mean Clint couldn't go.

"Mary!" Clint shouted.

She turned her head and looked at him. And she realized suddenly that she had no right to make this decision for him. She had no right to deny him the chance to defend his own—Sombrero— his son . . .

She turned back to the two horses determinedly. Slowly, an inch at a time, she approached them, talking soothingly. One of them halted and stood, trembling.

She reached him and her hand closed over the reins. Gripping them tightly she returned to Clint, leading the horse.

Clint hobbled to the animal, took the reins and prepared to mount, from the right side instead of the left. Mary steadied him as he put his right foot into the stirrup and hauled himself up.

There were tears in her eyes as she looked up at him. Her lips formed the words, "Be careful, Clint."

Then he whirled the horse and galloped out of the courtyard. He disappeared into the darkness, but she could hear his shout.

She whirled and ran into the house. She got the rifle, took cartridges for it from a drawer. She loaded it and went out onto the gallery. She didn't know if there would be anything she could do. But she would be ready if there was.

# 22

Morgan hesitated on the gallery for a moment. Clint would be all right. Mary was with him and the leg wound, while serious, had not been bad enough to endanger Clint's life unless infection set in.

He stared into the night, toward the fires

blazing among the adobe huts. All was confusion out there. Unless the men forgot the fires and concentrated on fighting off the attacking force . . .

He didn't know if they'd listen to him. Even if they did, he wasn't sure he was capable of directing the defense successfully. But he was Clint Morgan's son and Clint couldn't do it himself.

He ran across the courtyard. From several horses milling just outside, he caught one and swung to the saddle. He yelled, "Pete!" and galloped toward the burning adobe village.

Men were running there, carrying buckets. Women and children milled around uncertainly, some of them carrying possessions from the huts that had not yet caught from the others. As he approached, a group of the raiders galloped among them, firing, yelling triumphantly.

And behind Morgan . . . the fire that had been set at the rear wall of the main house was growing too . . .

The battle of Sombrero was already lost, he thought. The defenders, outnumbered anyway, had further reduced their effectiveness by dispersing to fight the fires in their homes.

Clint would have rallied them. Clint, strong and able to ride, might have turned defeat into victory. But Clint was neither strong nor able to ride. He was unconscious, helpless, dependent on others to do what he wanted to do himself.

Dependent upon Morgan. Dependent upon his son.

Morgan spurred the horse under him. The animal broke into a run. Maybe they wouldn't listen to him. But it wouldn't be because he didn't try.

He reached the burning houses. He yanked his horse to a plunging halt. He yelled at the men, but his voice was lost in the roar of flames crackling in the brush beneath the sod roofs of the houses, in the lean-to sheds at the rear of some of them . . . He stared helplessly for an instant, then yanked the gun from his belt and fired it into the air. He roared, "Pete! The rest of you! Get your horses and your guns! You'll never be able to put those fires out until you drive that damn bunch off!"

They paused for a moment in what they were doing to stare dumbly at him. Then, as dumbly, they turned away from him and went on with what they had been doing.

Morgan saw Pete Candelario running, a bucket filled with water in his hand. Pete flung it over the burning roof of his house and turned to go after another one. Morgan rode to him and blocked him with his horse. "Pete!" he shouted. "You're not going to save anything anyway! If Clint gets whipped you're not even going to have a home!"

Pete stared up at him. His face was black with

soot and there was an angry burn on one cheek. "Pete!" Morgan bawled. "Damn it, listen to me!"

The bucket in Pete's hand suddenly clattered to the ground. He turned his head and stared at his burning house. For the first time he seemed to realize that it was beyond saving.

He glanced back up at Morgan, doubt showing in his eyes. "All right!" Morgan yelled angrily. "So I'm not Clint! But I'm not quitting, either!"

Pete ran for a horse. He swung to the saddle. He rode among the men still battling the fires and yelled, "Forget the fires! We can build more houses! But there won't be anyplace to build 'em unless we drive that damn bunch off!"

The men began to gather. Those that could caught horses and mounted them. The others gathered around afoot.

Some of them were wounded, and many were burned. The clothing of a couple of them was smoldering. There weren't enough, Morgan realized. But there *had* to be enough. Because these few were all there were.

He realized too how ill-equipped he was to lead them against a force twice as strong as they. He'd never held a gun in his hand until he came here a few short days before.

He felt Pete's eyes on him and turned his head. Pete was staring at him in an odd way—the same way he had looked at him that first day in town. As though . . .

As though I was Clint Morgan's son, he thought.

That was it. And that would have to do. If Clint Morgan couldn't lead his men then he'd have to do it in Clint's place.

Right now the raiders were scattered. They were under no direct command. They were busy setting fires.

The moment they realized the defenders had regrouped, they'd regroup themselves. But there might be a little time before they did.

"Come on!" he yelled. "And stay together!"

He headed through the adobe village of the hands. He swept along its single street. Those of the men who were mounted kept pace with him. The others ran along behind.

On the far edge of the village he encountered several of the raiders running from house to house, torches in their hands, setting fires— inside and in the trash piled against the buildings at the rear.

They saw him coming, dropped their torches and ran for their horses. Morgan spurred his horse to cut them off.

At pointblank range, one fired up at him. He felt the heat of the muzzle blast, felt a burn along the side of his neck. Then his horse struck the man with his chest and flung him helplessly to the ground.

Cut off from their horses, the men took cover

behind buildings, firing from there. "Catch those horses!" Morgan bawled. "Take 'em back to the ones that're afoot!"

He glanced toward the buildings behind which the raiders had taken cover. They had stopped firing. He caught a glimpse of a couple of them running, retreating. "Hurry it up!" he yelled.

He sat his fidgeting horse, watching as they caught one after another of the raiders' mounts and led them back to the men who were still on foot.

The bunch they'd surprised setting fires would get back to the main group of raiders as quickly as they could. Then the whole bunch would make a united attack. Unless Morgan could mop them up before they had a chance to get together again.

All his men were mounted now. He led away at a hard run, still hoping to overtake the men on foot before they could reach the main group.

He rode through the village and back again without seeing any of them. He glanced uncertainly toward the house. Perhaps they already were inside. And if they were, now was the time to find it out.

Running his horse recklessly, he led them through the courtyard gate. No gunfire greeted them. There was only silence.

He made a circle of the courtyard and led them out again. He wondered if the raiders had quit, if they had gone back to town. It didn't seem likely. Not when everything was going their way.

He circled the house. The motion, the noise, the men at his back—all these things contributed to a sudden feeling of exhilaration. He felt stronger than he had in many days. Perhaps, he thought, the fight wasn't lost after all. If he could cut down the odds—even a little bit . . .

He and his men swept around the house, surprising four of the raiders setting another fire in brush dragged up against the house.

He raised his gun, sighted as carefully as he could from the horse's back, and fired. He missed cleanly.

Behind him, the men fanned out, pouring a concentrated fire into the bunched group of four. One man went down, hugging his belly. The other three broke and ran.

Morgan's men overran them savagely, chopping with gun barrels, firing at pointblank range. Two more men went down. The fourth stopped and raised his hands.

Pete rode to him and deliberately brought his gun down in a chopping motion. The man collapsed to the ground. Pete looked at Morgan and yelled, "We can't spare men to guard prisoners!"

The action had seemed unnecessarily brutal, but Morgan said nothing. Pete was right. Besides that, Morgan couldn't see that the raiders were entitled to much consideration. They weren't fighting for a principle. They were only after land and willing to kill and burn for it.

At a gallop, he led them around the corner of the house. He pulled his plunging horse instantly to a halt. Overcoming the four had been easy and had caused no loss among Morgan's men. But the easy victories were over. Just beyond the rim of illumination cast into the night by the burning house the remaining raiders had grouped and now milled, awaiting word from whoever was leading them to attack.

Morgan glanced at Pete and caught the man watching his face. Pete grinned faintly and immediately looked away. But by now, Morgan understood that look. He had again reminded Pete of Clint—perhaps of Clint a long, long time ago.

The men pulled up in a circle around him. He stared across the intervening space at the group of raiders. In a few minutes some of them were going to die. And some in Morgan's group would die.

Nor were the raiders likely to give up. Even if Morgan and his men managed to inflict heavy losses on them. They outnumbered the defenders by six or eight.

Morgan turned his head. "We'll ride through 'em. Then circle around and head for the court-yard gate. Maybe we can hold the place from there."

He waited just a moment, his stomach feeling as if it contained a ball of ice. "And yell," he said. "Yell as loud as you can."

He sank spurs into the horse's sides. The startled animal leaped ahead. Morgan stood in the stirrups, revolver upraised, as the horse surged into a steady run.

He opened his mouth and yelled, and behind him, Pete and the others howled like maniacs.

The raiders stared at them in surprise. A few glanced uneasily around as though expecting attack from behind. Morgan grinned briefly and yelled again. They couldn't believe he would attack head-on with as few men as he had. They thought there must surely be more attacking from the rear.

This belief among the raiders held them motionless, inactive long enough for Morgan and the others to close the distance separating them. Then Morgan was within range and brought his revolver down into line.

He fired, and behind him and to both sides, the guns of his men roared unevenly. Three men tumbled from their saddles ahead. The others broke, opening a path for Morgan to thunder through.

He saw their faces and then was through, still savagely spurring his running horse. "Two!" Pete howled exultantly. "By God, we got two more of 'em!"

Morgan drew slightly left, then sharply left, and headed back toward the house. The raiders, realizing they had been fooled, spurred their horses in pursuit. Morgan turned and fired over his shoulder, but the revolver only clicked.

He reached the gate, went through and leaped from his horse as the animal came to a plunging halt. He ran back toward the wall.

The others followed suit. Two of the raiders came through the gate and immediately drew the concentrated fire of the defenders. Both went down.

Morgan ran to the nearest one and snatched up his gun from the ground nearby. He ran back to the wall.

Pete Candelario was down, writhing at the base of the low wall. Another man was down, motionless. Still a third was staring at his arm, from which blood dripped steadily.

But the others were firing, regularly, carefully. And outside the wall the raiders were backing off . . .

The firing slacked and stopped. Morgan glanced swiftly around. He was down to eight men, not counting himself. And there must still be nearly twice that many in the attacking group.

He laid his gun on the top of the wall and knelt beside Pete Candelario. "Help me get my back against the wall," Pete said hoarsely.

Morgan dragged him the few feet to the wall

and settled him with his back to it. "Where is it?" he asked. "Is it bad?"

"Groin. God damn the bastards, another inch . . ."

Morgan couldn't help grinning at him. Pete had opened his pants and was looking at the wound, bloody and painful but not serious.

Morgan turned his head and stared beyond the wall. The fires in the adobe houses were dying now, having consumed most of what was burnable. The light was fading.

He wondered what time of night it was and when it would begin getting light. He admitted to himself that there wasn't much chance for them. They'd be pinned down here while the attackers sniped with rifles from the cover of the burned-out huts.

Unless help arrived . . . And who would help Sombrero? Who would help Clint Morgan or Clint Morgan's men?

No one, he supposed. But at least he was better off than he had been earlier tonight. At least he was still alive.

# 23

Clint Morgan rode out of the yard as Morgan led the men in their howling charge straight into the attackers' ranks. Instinctively his spurs sank themselves into the horse's sides as he prepared to join his son.

Almost immediately, he hauled the confused animal to a prancing halt. He stared at Morgan, who was standing in his stirrups and yelling like a crazy man. A tight grin of approval touched his mouth.

He could join his son, and wanted to. But he understood that the frontal attack was not intended as an all-out fight. It was a slashing raid, from which Morgan and the others would immediately retreat—probably to the protection of the house.

He further understood that once they were holed up in the house—outnumbered and weary—it would only be a matter of time until they were forced to surrender or killed.

Unless help arrived. But who would help? Who would help Sombrero?

No one, he admitted. Jaime Candelario wouldn't be able to raise a posse to fight Sombrero's battles. And even if Jaime had sent for troops, they couldn't possibly arrive in time.

The help would have to come from the people on Sombrero itself. Yet all the men were with Morgan, already fighting as hard as they could.

The men were. But what about their wives? He turned his head and stared toward the village of adobe huts.

Almost imperceptibly he shook his head. They couldn't help. They had no guns.

Between himself and the huddled group of women and children, his glance touched one of the dead raiders lying on the ground. A rifle lay nearby. Clint's eyes narrowed. There *were* guns. There were the guns of the dead and wounded, lying scattered wherever they had fallen.

He glanced once more, regretfully, toward the clashing forces a hundred yards away. Then he turned his horse and sank his spurs.

He clung to the saddle horn as pain and weakness washed over him. He galloped to the huddled group. "Your men are going to be killed unless you help," he shouted harshly. "Every dead man had a gun. Find them and get their guns. Then come back here."

They stared at him as though they did not comprehend. Then they scattered like startled quail.

The older children stayed with the little ones. Clint sat his horse silently, watching as Morgan and those with him slashed through the raiders, wheeled and headed for the house.

Already some of the women were returning, carrying rifles or revolvers or both. Morgan reached the courtyard gate and rode inside. There was a brief flurry of action, and a score of crackling shots. Then the raiders retreated out of rifle range.

The light from the burning adobe village was almost gone. There was light yet from the burning house, and that would grow stronger as more of the house was consumed. It would continue to illuminate the battle for a while.

No one seemed to be paying any attention to the women. They were returning now, some emptyhanded, some carrying guns. "A couple of you take the kids," Clint yelled. "Get them as far away as you can. The rest of you come with me."

He rode slowly toward the nearest adobe houses. He positioned the women in their shelter, so that they could fire toward the courtyard gate. So that all would understand, he spoke to them in Spanish. "Wait until they attack again. Then shoot as carefully as you can. If you can't hit the men, knock their horses down."

Afterward he waited impatiently for the charge he knew would come. He couldn't see the raiders, for they were beyond the circle of light cast by the burning house. But he could hear them wrangling. Anger and bitterness touched his eyes. Getting beaten would be bad enough.

But to get beaten by a bunch of malcontents like that, who would carve Sombrero into little pieces and then spend the rest of their lives haggling over the pieces . . .

The wrangling stopped. A voice, one he recognized as belonging to Nate Duffy, yelled, "Now! This time we'll clean 'em out for good!"

The thunder of hoofs began and they came out of the darkness into the light, spread out in a long line, headed straight for the house. This time they would make it inside, Clint thought. This time they knew exactly what they were up against. They'd put their horses over the wall and through the gate. They wouldn't bother doing much shooting until they were inside. Then their superior numbers would pay off.

On and on they came, looking like twice their number in the faint orange light. "Don't shoot until I tell you to," Clint said urgently. "Then shoot as fast as you can."

The women probably wouldn't hit anything, but it wasn't going to matter whether they did or not. The important advantage would come from the raiders' realization that they were in a crossfire. They wouldn't know the new force was composed of women. Not until it was too late.

The raiders reached a point between Clint and the house and veered toward the house.

"Now!" Clint yelled. "Give 'em everything you've got!"

Rifles and revolvers bellowed. A cloud of powder smoke drifted up from half a dozen guns. The second volley was ragged, and Clint added the sound of his own revolver to it.

Nor were the defenders at the house silent. Their guns crackled regularly, putting a deadly hail of lead into the attackers' ranks.

They weren't beaten yet, in spite of the three who had tumbled from their saddles. But, Clint thought, they didn't know they weren't. He rode out from behind the adobe building and sank his spurs. "Now, by God!" he yelled. "Get 'em! Don't let a damned one of 'em get away!"

He spurred toward them at a pounding run. Forgotten was his weakness and his wound.

And over at the house . . . half the defenders had thought him dead, or at least mortally wounded. Seeing him alive, strong, sitting the back of his horse and charging the attackers alone . . . It was the spark they needed to make them forget the odds.

Mounted, yelling, firing their guns, they rode out of the courtyard gate. Clint charged Duffy's bunch from one direction, Morgan and the men from the other. Duffy's bunch milled for a moment, then whirled their horses and fled.

Clint, Morgan, Pete, and the others thundered in pursuit. Two more men tumbled from the saddle. Then the sound of hoofs was dying away into the darkness, and Clint was pulling up.

Again he had to cling to the saddle horn. His head reeled and bright lights flashed before his eyes. He gritted his teeth and held on.

Beyond him by two hundred yards, the others pulled up. They rode back to him excitedly. Morgan caught him as he slipped sideways in his saddle. He steadied him while Pete Candelario dismounted and took the reins of Clint's horse.

Morgan swung from his saddle immediately. His own leg wound was stiff with clotted blood, and sore. Steadying Clint, he walked beside his father's horse toward the house.

It was over. He felt the tension drain suddenly out of him, leaving him dizzy and weak.

He heard the sound of hoofs, and tensed himself again, watching the darkness in the direction from which they came. It couldn't be the raiders returning, he thought. These sounds came from the opposite direction.

He saw three riders come into the circle of light and stop. One was smaller than the others . . .

He recognized them then. Jaime Candelario. Jaime's brother Juan. And Ellen . . .

The three saw him at almost the same instant. They rode toward him. Jaime and Juan dismounted and took over the job of steadying

Clint, one on each side. The men went on ahead to fight the fire in the house.

The wives of the hands threw down their guns and moved among the wounded and dead. Ellen stood very still, looking up into Morgan's face. "We thought . . . we were sure . . ." Tears glistened in her eyes. She swallowed and brushed at them with a hand. "You're hurt," she said.

"It's nothing serious." He followed along behind Clint's horse, with Ellen keeping pace. Jaime turned his head. "Where's Kehoe? Has he been here?"

Morgan nodded. "He's lying on the gallery. He's dead."

Jaime's expression was disappointed. "I was hoping . . . Oh well."

"Maybe . . . He might have told my mother about killing Parfet. He was with her when we arrived."

"Let's go see."

Morgan stopped as they entered the courtyard gate. He looked down into Ellen's upturned face. "I'm going to stay," he said. "I . . ." He wanted to put all the things he was feeling into words but he knew it was impossible. "I'll have to stand trial," he said.

Nothing had really changed, Morgan realized suddenly. The sheriff still had a warrant for his arrest. If he and Clint went to trial, they'd have no more chance now than they would have had before. Less chance, probably.

Jaime came out of the house. He stood in the doorway for a moment, lighted by reflection from the fire at the back of the house, but with his face in shadow. Morgan wished he could see it and the expression it held.

Jaime crossed the courtyard toward them. Behind him, Juan and Pete carried Clint into the house. Reaching them, Jaime said, "Kehoe killed Parfet all right. He bragged to Mary that he had."

Ellen's voice was very soft. "Do you think he really told her that?"

The sheriff shrugged. "I don't know and I don't want to know. Nobody's going to doubt her. Not Mary."

Morgan felt weak with relief as he went on. "That lets you and Clint off the hook. It puts Duffy and the rest of that bunch out there squarely in the wrong." He frowned faintly. "The courts are going to be busy in this county for a long, long time to come."

Morgan glanced at Ellen. There was sound in the air and noise. The shouting of the firefighters—the weeping of the women for their wounded and their dead—the groans of the wounded as they were moved . . .

But Ellen was smiling up at him. He put a hand out toward her and she met it halfway with her own.

He turned his head and glanced toward the sprawling adobe house. Even as it was now, half-consumed by fire, it did not seem forbidding. He wondered why it had ever seemed so to him. Right now it seemed like home.

| | | | |
|---|---|---|---|
| Books are produced in the United States using U.S.-based materials | Books are printed using a revolutionary new process called THINKtech™ that lowers energy usage by 70% and increases overall quality | Books are durable and flexible because of smythe-sewing | Paper is sourced using environmentally responsible foresting methods and the paper is acid-free |

## Center Point Large Print
600 Brooks Road / PO Box 1
Thorndike, ME 04986-0001 USA

**(207) 568-3717**

**US & Canada:**
**1 800 929-9108**
www.centerpointlargeprint.com